T0319143

beautiful disaster

Also by Kylie Adams

Bling Addiction
Book 2 in the Fast Girls, Hot Boys series

Cruel Summer
Book 1 in the Fast Girls, Hot Boys series

beautiful disaster

kylie adams

a
*fast girls,
hot boys*
novel

MTV BOOKS

POCKET BOOKS   MTV BOOKS
New York   London   Toronto   Sydney

POCKET BOOKS, a division of Simon & Schuster, Inc.
1230 Avenue of the Americas, New York, NY 10020

ISBN-13: 978-1-4165-2042-9
ISBN-10:   1-4165-2042-2

This MTV Books/Pocket Books trade paperback edition November 2006

10   9   8   7   6   5   4   3   2   1

Manufactured in the United States of America

For information regarding special discounts for bulk purchases,
please contact Simon & Schuster Special Sales at 1-800-456-6798
or business@simonandschuster.com.

For Wendy Shenefelt—
gorgeous, hilarious, and a whip-smart supergirl
who knows how to work the system . . .

Live fast, die young,
and leave a good-looking corpse.

—James Dean

beautiful disaster

From: Bijou

If there's anything sadder than seeing a life snuffed
out before its time, then I haven't encountered it yet.

10:21 pm 5/26/06

prologue

"how should we respond to a tragedy like this?"

Bijou Ross, valedictorian, Class of 2006, posed the question to her fellow graduates of the Miami Academy for Creative and Performing Arts. She sized up the crowd, her anxiety giving way to anger.

"Should we post photographs of the dead body on Facebook-dot-com?"

The audience had been quiet. Now they were more quiet.

"There's only one reaction to the senseless act that we witnessed last night . . . and that's to never forget it. Anyone of us could've been the victim. We're here today because fate spared us. Luck intervened. God had another plan. Don't take that for granted. Use it. Cherish it. And above all else . . . *respect* it."

Bijou paused a beat, staring out into the auditorium, scanning the sea of somber faces. They were young, but the crack of that fatal gunshot and its blood-soaked aftermath had aged all of them overnight. And it showed.

"Examine your own commitments to yourself, to your future, to the people in your life. Make them meaningful. Live, embrace, and hold dear what's important to you . . . while you have it. The takeaway from this nightmare is that we're all fragile. Youth guarantees us nothing. So don't waste a moment of it."

And with that, Bijou stepped away from the podium, returning to her seat on the stage. She was positioned next to headmaster Timothy J. Heimer, who gave her a serious nod and mouthed the words, "Good job."

At first, an uncomfortable silence boomed—mere seconds in total, but interminable just the same. But then came a thunderous ovation of applause.

Bijou zeroed in on the crowd. Down there, among the throngs of MACPA graduates, stood the school's fabulous five . . . *minus one*. The absence was so conspicuous that the missing person stood out like neon—a palpable, second-by-second reminder that only last night there were 112 seniors scheduled to glide across the stage to collect their diplomas. But this morning that number had become 111.

Bijou watched the remaining four clasp hands. No doubt they were relying on one another for strength to endure the reality of sudden violence, to deal with the survivor's guilt, to get through the ceremony without breaking down altogether.

Vanity St. John.

Max Biaggi Jr.

Pippa Keith.

Dante Medina.

Christina Perez.

Those five students were nothing if not notorious. But not all of them would be taking that walk across the stage to end one chapter in life . . . and to begin another. Only four names would be called.

Because somebody was dead.

Headmaster Heimer approached the podium. He cleared his throat of emotion. "Class of 2006, please rise . . ."

From: Dante

Vanity's gone. Her room's trashed.
I've got a bad feeling, man.

1:09 am 4/09/06

chapter one

spring break of senior year

max Biaggi Jr. paced the waiting area of New York University Medical Center, his booze buzz long gone. Nothing like the adrenaline of white-hot fear to kick in instant sobriety.

He was the son of Hollywood's hottest action star, Miami's most celebrated party promoter, and, at seventeen, already had a list of sexual conquests approaching that triple-digit figure with a one and two zeros. But right now he was just an older brother, praying for God to spare the life of his baby sister.

A soft touch grazed his arm. "I'm going to get a cup of coffee. Can I get you some?"

Max looked at Bethany with a savage intensity. She was a girl he'd met at the Tar Beach rooftop party practically five minutes ago. They were supposed to be in his hotel suite having sex, not in a hospital lobby sweating out life-or-death news.

"I don't need coffee, bitch. I just need to know that my sister's going to make it." And then Max sank down into a chair and began nervously chewing on the nail of his index finger.

For a long moment, Bethany just stood there, speechless, her face a masterpiece of hurt and embarrassment.

Max ignored her.

Finally, she walked away.

He would never see her again. Like he gave a shit. Bethany was just some party skank he wanted to nail. And suddenly she wanted an upgrade to instant girlfriend who provides emotional support in a moment of crisis? Thanks, but no thanks, baby.

Once more, Max put his Sidekick II to work calling his friends—Vanity, Dante, Pippa, and Christina. And once again, not one of them answered.

Max was alone. He was scared as hell, too. "Come on, Sho," he murmured. "Don't go out like this. That would make me an orphan."

A young Asian woman in surgical scrubs approached, her expression severe and disapproving. "You brought in Shoshanna Biaggi?"

Max stood quickly, nodding as he took in the badge that announced her as Dr. Elizabeth Tang. "I'm her brother. Is she—"

"Are you the one who gave her the drugs?"

"N-no . . . of course not," Max stammered.

"So—what?" Dr. Tang countered in a caustic tone. "You just stood there and watched her take them?"

Max knew that his expression was almost pleading. "No, like I told the paramedics . . . she was hanging with this guy who makes his own chem shit. He swears he didn't give her anything, but I know he's lying—"

Dr. Tang raised an impatient hand to silence him. "She was given—or rather she took—*something*. At this point, my best guess is a dangerously high dose of PCP, but it'll take a few days for the toxicology report to come back. And it might not reveal much."

"How is she?" Max asked.

Dr. Tang betrayed no emotion. "Your sister's in a coma." One beat. "I suggest you call your parents. They need to get here as soon as possible."

Max's mind got stuck on the last bit. "Are you saying she's going to die?" The question croaked out faintly, no more than a whisper.

"The next few hours are critical," Dr. Tang said gravely. "And it could go either way. So like I said—call your parents."

Max watched her disappear, struggling to maintain his composure as he glanced around. He hated the democracy of hospital emergency rooms—rich, poor, gorgeous, ugly, brilliant, uneducated. The same care and effort went into saving all of them. For once, all of his Hollywood name dropping and trust-fund power didn't mean a goddamn thing.

The guilt began to gnaw away at him like a flesh-eating virus. If only he had told Shoshanna no. If only he had listened to that instinct deep inside telling him that making a mark on the Manhattan party scene *and* watching over his sister was an impossible spring break agenda. But Max had convinced himself that he could do it, rationalizing that his sister was more likely to find trouble alone in Miami than with her brother in New York. He felt a stab of self-loathing: Great call, Superboy.

Shoshanna was a true wild child—fifteen going on twenty-one. She showcased her breast implants to eye-popping effect, always assumed a provocative, vampish fashion style, and frequently put herself in the path of older guys who wanted only one thing from her. The girl was an impossible princess. But Max loved that openly defiant, potty-mouthed bitch-brat like no one else in the world.

Call your parents.

Max stared down at his Sidekick, dreading the task. He dialed his father first. It started to ring. "Pick up the phone, you son of a bitch . . ."

I don't kiss whores . . .

Pippa Keith was lost in a foggy tableau, vaguely aware of the horror, yet still feeling like it was happening to someone else. A total free fall from fairy tale to nightmare. How could it be? In answer to the confusion, her body was in a strange state of paralysis.

Just minutes ago she had been living the almost perfect fantasy. A private date on a private plane with Max Biaggi, the ultimate Hollywood superstar—handsome, charismatic, sexy . . . and megarich.

Max the son was a boy, but Max the father was a man. And that difference had been incredible enough for her to play the dangerous game, of keeping her job a secret from her best mate and keeping her true identity a secret from her future husband.

It was a double life. By day she was Pippa, the new girl from England who dominated the theater department at the Miami Academy for Creative and Performing Arts. By night she was Star Baby, the refreshingly classy, talented dancer who ruled the stage at Cheetah, the strip club that provided the setting to make mountains of money *and* entertain men of means in an upstairs VIP room called "The Lair."

One of those men had been Max Biaggi, and Pippa had fallen hard, fast, and blindly for him, mistaking their many private sessions for a real relationship. Oh God, how could a girl be so wrong? Her presence tonight had nothing to do with an actual date and everything to do with a crude transaction. It was between Max Biaggi, Cheetah's top patron, and Vinnie Rossetti, Cheetah's tough manager. A simple cash deal.

I own you, Star Baby.

Max Biaggi's voice ricocheted inside Pippa's mind as he pinned her down. She was facedown on the stateroom bed as the private jet flew to some destination unknown.

Vinnie charged me top dollar for you, and I expect to get my money's worth.

The replay of the cruel words blistered and burned as Pippa lay there, emotionally wrecked, prepared to submit to any humiliation, if only to bring this nightmare to a faster end.

What a bloody fool she was . . . to believe even for a moment that she was anything more to this bastard than a commodity of flesh—a private dance to buy, a private date to broker. And to think that only minutes ago Pippa had been building castles in the air, imagining a future, a marriage, a life together . . . with *him*.

Pippa could feel Max Biaggi's hands pushing up the Gucci wrap dress. It was past her waist now. She shut her eyes, recoiling from his touch as hot tears rolled down her cheeks.

"Just think, Star Baby, after this you'll be an official member of the Mile High Club." His voice was thick with lust, his breathing uneven.

Pippa grimaced as she heard the distinct sound of a zipper going down . . . and after that, the crinkling of a Mylar-wrapped condom being ripped open. "Please . . . don't . . ."

"I thought a whore like you would be begging for it." He hissed into her ear, then darted his tongue in and out before giving her lobe a playful bite, his teeth crunching slightly on her H. Stern chandelier earrings.

Pippa struggled to shift her body from underneath him, but Max Biaggi's hold was too firm. Even her strongest effort proved futile.

"Why'd you get so dressed up, Star Baby? Did you think I was going to take you out and show you off?" He started to laugh as his hand began peeling down her underwear. "I've got an image to protect. Cheetah girls are just a dirty little secret." He slapped the right cheek of her butt with the palm of his hand.

Pippa experienced the loud pop and the sharp sting simultaneously, and the humiliation triggered a quiet, simmering rage. Once more, she fought to get free.

But Max Biaggi tightened his grip. "What do I have here—another Hellcat? Do you want to wrestle? Is that what you want? Or do you just like it a little rough?" He gave her hair a vicious tug.

Pippa winced in pain. This date was supposed to be her night of romance. This man was supposed to be her dream guy. It seemed impossible that everything had gone so wrong. Yet here she was, living out loud the horrifying reality.

Max Biaggi had straddled her and locked Pippa's body between his knees in a vise-tight hold. But the strongest part of her remained free . . . her legs. Yes. Her long, lean dancer's legs. Miss Bill, MACPA's musical theater director, had been relentless, grinding her through Broadway boot camp to get her ready for the challenging choreography of *Sweet Charity*. That, coupled with her pole routines at Cheetah, had built up impressive leg strength and also made her incredibly limber.

Pippa bucked in protest as Max Biaggi roughly finger probed the forbidden part of her.

All of a sudden, the voice of Hellcat roamed around Pippa's mind like a wolf in the woods.

Don't be surprised if he only gives it to you in the ass. He says that saves him from she's-having-my-baby scams. Trust me, I've been where you're going tonight.

Pippa shut her eyes as the vile truth became painfully

clear. She had considered herself so far above Hellcat, also a stripper at Cheetah and her most ferocious rival, yet they were living the same sordid life, even suffering the same cruel treatment at the hands of a Hollywood hero.

"Are you ready for me, Star Baby?" Max Biaggi breathed.

"Please stop!" Pippa cried, her voice shaking with emotion.

Max Biaggi laughed. "Do you really mean that? Because I don't think that you do."

Pippa could feel his arousal, right there at her opening. Beneath him she squirmed violently, trying desperately to break free.

"I think you want it. I think you want it *bad*. You're a whore. I'm a movie star. This is the best thing that'll ever happen to you. So just relax and enjoy it."

Pippa's emotions ran up and down the scale. But a sudden ferocious anger seemed more powerful than all of her other feelings combined.

She shot out her right leg—foot arched to deliver the Manolo Blahnik spike heel first—kicking back, up, and then in toward her body.

Thwack.

Pippa felt and heard the stiletto heel make direct contact with Max Biaggi's skull.

The sick bastard grunted in agony.

Again, Pippa fought to get out from under him, and

this time she won the battle, twisting, squirming, and rolling until free. Her feet were on the cabin floor now.

She could make a run for it . . .

Christina Perez experienced the most placid calm as she went down, falling from the rooftop ledge, sailing midair to the death that would soon belong to her.

I would rather you commit suicide than live that life.

The words of her mother, Paulina Perez, a right-wing conservative and a politician with a bloodlust for the power of a Senate seat, echoed in Christina's mind. Instead of allowing her to be honest about her sexual orientation and live openly as a lesbian, the woman who gave birth to Christina would rather she drop dead.

Congratulations, Mommy. I am, she thought.

Christina's body felt limp and weightless, as if nothing but a mere rag doll. It had been dulled to zombielike inertia from too many hits of the vodka bong. Scenes from the party flashed in her mind. Tar Beach. Max's big New York rooftop bash. And the kiss . . . that wonderful, terrible kiss.

Vanity St. John, the gorgeous, famous-for-being-famous teen celebutante, the headline queen who relegated Paris Hilton to media irrelevancy, the girl Christina loved from afar, had kissed her. And not just a platonic girl-to-girl peck. It had been a real kiss, a lover's kiss, full of passion and desire. And it had also been a joke. The cackling laughter that followed was proof of that, as had been the words, so cavalier, so unintentionally mean . . .

God, I'm so drunk! You're a good kisser, though. One day you'll make some girl very happy.

An easy sentiment to slur. But an impossible one to fathom. For Christina, the notion of "some girl" did not exist. There was only "a girl" . . . Vanity. The evidence of her dedication was on display in Christina's art, *Harmony Girl*, the *manga* she had slavishly created in tribute to Vanity, every illustration, every panel, every scripted word fueled by her crush. To have that depth of feeling thoughtlessly dismissed and toyed with . . . well, the only cruelty to compare it to was her mother's.

Everything seemed to be happening in frame-by-frame slow motion. It was only seconds ago that Christina had been standing on the building's ledge, peering down, contemplating a jump, a way out of her miseries, in only the slightest hypothetical sense.

But it happened anyway. The danger of a single slip combined with her alcohol-induced slow reflexes had seen to that. And now she was falling . . . down . . . to the end that would be her body hitting the concrete below.

Suddenly, Christina experienced a violent jolt, her left leg absorbing most of the impact as she slammed shoulderfirst against the brick building.

The shock of the moment countervailed the pain.

Christina swung this way and that way, like a pendulum. She glanced up to see the string from the Christmas lights wrapped noose-tight around the ankle and heel of her boot. And then all motion stopped. She just hung there, precariously suspended over a death drop.

She screamed her throat raw, desperate to compensate for the party music and the sounds of the city night. Would anyone hear her? And how long could the electrical wire hold without breaking?

Dante Medina stared at the message painted in blood that defaced Vanity's hotel bathroom mirror.

A DIRTY BITCH WUZ HERE

He just shook his head, overcome with incredulity. A short time ago Dante and Vanity had been arguing at Max's Tar Beach rooftop party. But maybe that was the wrong word for it. Vanity was drunk and lashing out. Dante had been reacting.

That's all he ever did in relation to Vanity. React to being the son of a maid in the presence of the famous rich girl. React to being kicked out of her speedboat and left to drown. React to being screwed over by her father's recording label. Shit. When it came down to *reacting*, Dante Medina had reached his goddamn limit.

So he had switched to offensive mode, determined to

announce his feelings, no matter how jumbled they were. Because in spite of everything, he actually loved that beautiful, mixed-up girl.

Dante had followed her back to the hotel, only to find Vanity missing. Her door was ajar. The place was trashed. Hotel security had been his first call. Two men turned up with accusations disguised as questions. Apparently, Vanity had caused a scene at the downstairs bar when refused a drink. They clearly thought all of this was the work of an angry drunk.

A DIRTY BITCH WUZ HERE

But not that. He touched the mirror again, then inspected the blood on his finger. This discovery in the bathroom changed everything. It upgraded a cause for concern into a red-alert emergency.

Dante pivoted, stepping back into the main room to address the W Hotel's assistant manager and security guard. "Look at this."

They followed Dante's lead, trading blank stares after taking in the disturbing image.

And then Dante launched into a rant. "This isn't some crazy drunk girl acting out. Something happened here. Something *bad*. If you believe that she's still on the property, then I want every room in this hotel searched. I want security videos reviewed. I want—"

"Young man—"

"Don't patronize me with your 'young man' bullshit," Dante fumed, cutting off the assistant manager two words into his lame-ass spiel. "Anything less than treating this like the emergency that it is will mean instant PR problems for you, dude. Her publicist will get this joint in the headlines. But not for reasons that'll make corporate proud."

Dante picked up on the alarm in the manager's eyes the moment the word "publicist" dropped. And then he decided to motivate him even more. "She's famous, she's beautiful, and she's seventeen. Do the headline math."

The manager turned to the security guard. "Call nine-one-one."

Slowly, Vanity came up from the deep, unconsciousness lifting like a fog. She experienced the vague sensation of being alert. And then a wave of nausea hit. Worse than any hangover.

Her body lurched violently. On reflex, she attempted to cover her mouth with her hand. But the movement met with painful resistance.

Oh God! Both arms were tied to the bed frame with thick rope that burned her wrists when she tugged for freedom. Her feet were tied down, too. She was spread-eagled. Immobilized. Vulnerable. Defenseless.

Shock and confusion overrode her physical urge to vomit. Terror ruled, leeching the heat from her body. She began to shiver and fought to reclaim the memory of the lost hours.

Where was she? How long had she been here? Who had done this? What was going to happen to her?

Vanity worked herself into such a state of distress that a film of sweat slicked her from head to toe. Tears rolled down her cheeks. Why couldn't she remember?

She screamed. And not just any scream. It was a wail of despair and frustration, a plea for release, a begging for mercy.

Suddenly, she heard music. Loud music. The thrash-metal assault drowned out her cries and ramped up her fears.

Megadeth's "Symphony of Destruction." The song choice was a dead giveaway. Vanity's heart pounded in a stutter beat as one thing became clear: who had done this to her.

It was no longer a question. Because now she knew the answer.

From: Max

Is everybody wasted? WTF??? Holler back!

1:31 am 4/09/06

chapter two

Max knew this much about his mother: She went by the name Angela Everhart; she lived in a five-bedroom penthouse in one of Donald Trump's high-rises; and she had two young sons, Reeves and Thomas . . . which automatically made them Max's half brothers.

But he didn't even know what they looked like. Angela had always discouraged his interest to visit, and she never mailed the pictures that she always promised to send.

Sometimes it was easier to blame the new husband for her emotional freeze-out. After all, Robert Everhart, a defense attorney with an uncanny knack for taking on the most lurid, high-profile cases, had to be a cold-hearted bastard. How else could he defend wife murderers, baby killers, and child molesters?

Three rings went by before a groggy yet startled female voice picked up. "Hello?"

"Mom, it's Max. I'm sorry, I know it's late."

"Max? What time is it? What's wrong?" Her questions were hushed.

"I'm in New York with Sho. She's in the hospital." All of a sudden, Max experienced a crashing wave of pent-up anguish. He broke down. "She's . . . she's in a coma."

"What happened?"

"We were at a party." Max barely managed to get the words out through the tears. "They think it's a reaction to a club drug or something."

"It's okay, sweetheart . . ."

Max's heart swelled at the sound of his mother's comforting words . . . and then deflated when he realized that she wasn't talking to him.

"Go back to sleep," Angela went on. "It's just a late-night crisis. I'll be off in a minute." There was a long pause. "Where are you, Max? Which hospital?"

"NYU Medical Center."

"Have you spoken to your father?"

"I can't find him."

"Of course not." She sniffed bitterly. "I'll come by in the morning, after I get the boys to school."

At first, Max couldn't believe it. "So you're not coming *now*?" He knew that his voice was brimming with hurt and anger.

"Robert's in the middle of a big trial," Angela explained. "I can't disrupt his schedule, and I don't want to upset the boys. I'll get them to school and then come straight there."

Max could only feel a tight fight-or-flight sensation in his chest. He was ready to explode. "You don't want to 'disrupt his schedule'? Fuck his schedule! Your only daughter is in a goddamn coma! Or don't you give a shit?"

"Don't ever speak to me like that again," Angela hissed. "How did she end up in a coma in the first place? Where were you when your sister was doing drugs? Chasing some slut?"

Max said nothing.

"You're just like your father. You look like him. You sound like him. It's disgusting."

"Well, I didn't choose the son of a bitch," Max shot back. "*You* did. You married him, you screwed him, and you gave birth to his children. So don't blame me. I didn't have a say about either one of my worthless parents." Max didn't know what surprised him more—that he'd actually uttered those words out loud, or that it felt so good to say them.

"Don't—"

He cut her off. "No, *you* don't, Mom. I'm killing myself with guilt already, and the last thing I need is for you—of all people—to try and pour on more. You haven't been there for Sho. Not at all. I try to look out for her, but

I can't be her mother and her father. I'm only seventeen, and you want to blame *me*? You won't even deviate from your precious family routine to come see about your dying daughter, but you still want to blame me. This family is fucked!"

When he finished, Angela made no attempt to fill the silence. Finally, she broke it. "I'll get there as soon as I can." And then she hung up.

Max knew that meant tomorrow, after her husband had been sufficiently pampered, after her children—the ones she actually chose to mother—had been safely delivered to their elite school.

He sat down on one of the cheap faux-leather sofas. Alone. He waited for news that didn't come. Alone. And he prayed for Shoshanna to pull through. Because if she died, then that's exactly what Max would be for the rest of his life.

Alone.

Pippa's great escape took her no farther than the stateroom door.

Max Biaggi crashed into her body just as her trembling hand reached the knob. He pinned her against the wall and forced her thighs apart with his knee. "Where do you think you're going?"

Pippa shut her eyes.

He pressed against her, grinding into her, his breathing intensifying. "I can get plenty rough, Star Baby. I don't think you can handle it, though. You're too fragile."

An internal thunderbolt hit Pippa, triggering a frisson of pure hope. "Most seventeen-year-old girls are." The words spilled out, as if by divine inspiration.

Max Biaggi became statue-still. "What did you say?" He loosened his grip on her wrists as his question entered the stale cabin air.

Pippa twisted around to face him, her eyes gleaming with bitter triumph. "You heard me."

His eyes blazed into hers, probing, questioning, factoring in the possibility.

"Raping your son's classmate might not be the best career move," Pippa said. "But I'm no expert. Maybe you should run that idea by your agent first."

Max Biaggi's lips fell into a firm, tight line. "You're lying."

"Am I?" Pippa was practically taunting him now. "Your hard-on is fading. That must mean you're a little bit scared that I'm telling the truth."

"This is bullshit." He attempted to deliver the line action-hero tough, but there was the faintest hint of panic in the timbre of his voice.

Pippa glared at him, suddenly feeling more in control of the situation. "Is it bullshit that you live on Star Island? Because I've been to your son's parties."

His mouth twisted into a cruel smile. "What'd you do? Pick up *Star* magazine? Every awe-struck fan knows I have a house there."

"Does every fan know about Max Junior's poker games in the basement?"

His eyes narrowed.

"Or about the breast implants that you bought for Shoshanna on her fifteenth birthday?"

His smug smile was wiped clean.

And Pippa thundered on. "What about your wife Faith's thirst for martinis in the afternoon? Did I get that from *Star* magazine, too?"

Now it was Max Biaggi's turn to look scared. "Who the hell are you?"

"Just a girl," Pippa whispered, her tone at once coy and demonic. "Not old enough to vote . . . but young enough to ruin your life."

The bad-ass movie star was officially rattled now. Beads of sweat sprouted along his brow.

She began to sing "If My Friends Could See Me Now," then stopped cold. "I performed that in the MACPA spring production of *Sweet Charity*. Ask your son. He was there. You didn't bother to show up, though. I guess he's right when he says you suck as a father." She pulled up her underwear and adjusted her dress.

Max Biaggi drew back abruptly, his face a masterpiece of paranoia. "Did Vinnie put you up to this?"

Pippa mocked him with a smile. "Relax. This isn't an episode of *Twenty-four*. There's no conspiracy. Vinnie thinks I'm legal."

Max Biaggi shook his head with disgust. "You're a manipulative little bitch."

Pippa shrugged diffidently. "Can you blame me? Taco Bell uniforms are scratchy, and the take-home pay is shit."

Max Biaggi winced in pain. With his right hand, he rubbed the back of his head, only to discover blood on his fingertips. "You stupid underage whore! I'm bleeding!"

Pippa, hardly able to conjure up sympathy for his injury, made a show out of inspecting her high-flying Manolo Blahnik. "None of it got on my shoe, thank God." She glanced up at him, feeling almost powerful, the fear in her heart now replaced with disgust . . . and a hurt that she hoped would fade fast. "By the way, now might be a good time to tell the pilot we're going back to Miami."

"Be perfectly still!" a male voice called out. "I'm going to bring you up nice and easy. Just stay calm, girl. Stay calm."

Christina shut her eyes, obeying the stranger's words, surrendering completely to his nick-of-time rescue. She could feel the vague sensation of being pulled upward.

With each movement, his words loomed with greater clarity.

"That's it. You're doing great. Everything's going to be okay."

Closer.

"Almost there. Just a little more to go."

Closer.

"Gotcha!"

A firm hand gripped one leg, then the other, and in one fluid movement, he pulled her up to the ledge. Only then did Christina open her eyes.

It was him again—the Abercrombie ad come to life, the guy she had bumped into just minutes before her fall, the one who looked rich, handsome, and chiseled in the manner of an Ivy League star athlete.

He flashed a brilliant, hunky smile. "A fat girl would be dead right now. How much do you weigh? Eighty pounds?"

"Ninety-four," Christina managed to say. And then she proceeded to vomit all over him.

He stood there, frozen with repulsion.

Christina was mortified. The sickness had come without warning. Too much vodka, a kiss out of nowhere from Vanity St. John, a near-death experience, and hanging upside down could do that to a girl.

Physical relief lasted mere nanoseconds, quickly replaced by a punishing nausea. In apology, a meek groan was all she could muster.

The Ivy League knight stared down at his soiled clothes—a Rebel Yell DON'T SWEAT THE TECHNIQUE T-shirt and a ragged pair of 1921 jeans. "The word 'gross' comes to mind."

Christina lurched, feeling an unstoppable need to hurl again, only this time she twisted away at the last possible moment, just missing her savior's shiny new Pumas.

He peeled off his shirt and used the dry side to wipe off his jeans. Then he chucked it into a corner, standing there shirtless on the rooftop, revealing the kind of natural muscular definition that lesser male mortals could never find in the gym, no matter how hard they tried.

"FYI—if you throw up on me again, I'm tying that string of lights around your boot and tossing you back over the ledge." His tone was teasing yet gentle.

Christina smiled faintly, still reeling from the nausea. A light-headed sensation came over her, and she eased her way down to a sitting position.

He crouched to his knees and helped steady her as she dipped to one side. "I saved your life, and you puked on me. We should at least introduce ourselves. I'm Carb Duffy."

Christina regarded him for a moment, temporarily stunned by his phenomenal good looks and impossibly cut abdominals. "*Carb?*"

"It's a nickname that stuck. My buddies used to crack on me all the time, because whenever I drank a carbonated soda, I'd belch like a motherfu—"

Weakly, Christina raised a hand to stop him. The mere idea of a Mountain Dew, the simple thought of a burp, was almost enough to do her in.

Carb busied himself with the string of lights, unlooping it from around a heavy ceramic planter and rolling it into a tight circle. "Maybe you want to keep these," he suggested. "You know, for sentimental reasons."

"I'm Christina," she murmured. "Christina Perez." She paused a beat. "So *Carb* . . . are you simple or complex?"

He grinned, appreciating her clever play on words. "*Very* complex. Don't let the pretty-boy package fool you. Oh, shit, here we go again . . ."

And then Christina lost it, hurling once more, retching out her guts until it felt like she had no stomach lining left. By the end, she was cold, exhausted, and sweating profusely.

"You don't drink a lot, do you?" Carb asked.

Wearily, Christina tilted her head upward. "Try never."

"So what made you go hard-core?" His interest seemed sincere.

Christina took in a deep breath. The final purge brought with it the looming sensation that the worst of the alcohol sickness was behind her . . . and the twisted sobriety that the worst of her life was still in front of her. "My mother is sending me to a treatment center in Mississippi that promises to 'de-gay' teenagers."

"That's some heavy shit," Carb remarked. "It certainly explains the drinking and the jumping."

"I didn't jump," Christina murmured. "I thought about it . . . but I didn't do it." She glanced over at the ledge in question, shivering slightly. "I slipped."

The expression on Carb's face told her that he harbored serious doubt about her version of the truth. "Well, the next time you 'slip,' do what most girls do: swallow a few pills, and then call someone to tell them what you did."

"I'm not suicidal," Christina insisted.

"Maybe you are, but you're just not fully committed to it."

She looked at him. "Who *are* you?"

"Carb Duffy. Pay attention. We've already been over that. Now if you don't mind my opinion, this de-gay camp isn't worth a nine-story jump. Just refuse to go. Tell your mom to eat shit and die."

Christina shook her head. "You don't know my mother." She rolled her eyes. "Or maybe you do. She's running for a Florida Senate—"

Carb stopped her. "*Paulina Perez* is your mother?"

Christina nodded.

"And you're the girl who created that *manga* using Vanity St. John as a model? What's it called?"

"*Harmony Girl*," Christina replied quietly.

"Yeah, that's right, *Harmony Girl*." Carb regarded her strangely. "Your artwork knocked me out. You shouldn't be jumping off buildings. You should be—"

"I didn't jump!" Christina cried out in amused frustration. "God! You're driving me crazy!"

"Crazy enough to jump again?" Carb joked.

"As a matter of fact, *yes*." Christina laughed.

Carb laughed, too. "What are you doing in New York? I take it you still live in Florida."

She nodded. "Miami. I'm here on spring break with some friends."

"So maybe you should stay," Carb suggested. "Hang out in the city for a while."

Christina just sat there. He made it sound so easy. And they all made it look so easy—Vanity, Dante, Max, and Pippa—doing whatever they wanted with no maniac parent scrutinizing their every move. "You mean run away?"

If necessary, the staff of Salvation Pointe will come to this house and take you by force. And it's not kidnapping when your mother signs the consent form.

She played back Paulina's threat in her mind, recalling the determination in her eyes, the conviction in her voice. There was no escaping this. Christina felt cornered, like a wounded animal.

"I don't mean 'run away,' " Carb clarified. "It doesn't have to be a Lifetime movie. Just stay somewhere else until things calm down."

"My mother would consider that running away," Christina said helplessly.

"Well, I've got a place in Chelsea if you change your mind. It's small but nice. I'm a neat freak. Chances are I won't even be there. Tomorrow I head out to L.A. and after that D.C. and Miami."

His travel plans intrigued her. "That sounds like an exciting way to live. What do you do?"

Carb hesitated. "Since I'm wearing your vomit, I feel like I can tell you the truth." But then he looked at her, as if still deciding.

Now Christina was more intrigued. "What? Are you some kind of spy?"

"No, but it's a job that requires almost as much discretion." One beat. "I'm an escort."

For a moment, the true meaning didn't register. But then it did. "So women pay you for . . ."

Carb nodded. "And men, too. Mostly men, actually."

Christina was stunned. "What's the difference between an escort and a . . ."

Carb filled in the blank that she didn't want to say out loud. "Prostitute?"

Christina bit down on her lower lip, nodding guiltily, hoping that she hadn't offended him.

"You can't get me by the hour," Carb explained. "People pay me for companionship—special evenings out, weekends, vacations. If sex occurs, then it's the result of two consenting adults making that decision. It doesn't always happen. One of my regular clients is high up in the Pentagon. That's why I'm going to D.C. We've never even kissed. He just likes to hold my hand while we watch war movies on DVD at his townhouse in Georgetown. Of course, we're usually just wearing our underwear."

Christina laughed.

Carb laughed, too. "I know. It's weird. But he's a sweet guy."

"So if you see men and women, then you must be . . ."

"Bi, yeah. At the end of the day, I like thin blondes with big tits and dominant jocks along the lines of rugby and lacrosse players. Sexually, I'm all over the map."

Christina just stared at him, instantly reminded of her first encounter with Keiko, the Japanese girl who had been so radically honest about being a lesbian. Now Carb was making these bold announcements.

She wondered if there would ever be a day when she could speak this openly. To Christina, sexuality was still such a private subject. It was why she channeled all of her erotic energy into the creation of *Harmony Girl.* Dealing with the issue through her art seemed like the safest way to explore it.

In Christina's *manga*, the title character lived in an enchanted forest filled with magical animals, and she communicated with them only through music. The plot focused on a romantic triangle involving Harmony Girl's love for a dashing prince and her growing feelings for a young female artist named Lychee, who made secret trips from her village to the forest in order to obsessively sketch Harmony Girl's portrait.

"I'm serious about my apartment," Carb was saying. "It's yours if you want it."

Christina massaged her temples with her fingertips, feeling more punishment from the vodka binge coming on, this time in the form of a headache. She gave him a fuzzy look, puzzled by his instant trust and generosity. "But you barely know me."

"Well, I'd say we're fairly intimate. I saved your life, and you threw up on me."

She considered the point, smiling. "This is true."

"Just think about it. You don't have to tell me now."

A strong yearning to defy Paulina came over Christina. But something held her back. She just wasn't ready to strike out with such rebellion, and this realization filled her with a deep sense of shame. It was a shame that would prevent her from telling any of her friends where she was going. Salvation Pointe would be her pathetic secret to keep.

All of a sudden, Christina realized that the music had stopped. She rose up, peering beyond Carb to see that only a few stragglers remained on what had once been Tar

Beach, the ultimate rooftop event. It seemed odd. Max's parties usually lasted all night long. "What happened to everybody?"

Carb leveled a serious look. "A drug overdose tends to clear the room."

Christina blanched.

"Gorgeous girl," he went on. "Somebody said she was only fifteen. When the paramedics took her away, she was in rough shape."

A terrible fear registered as Christina's mind whirled with the vague recollection of hearing Max scream his sister's name just before the fall. "Oh my God. Was it Shoshanna Biaggi?"

Carb nodded in confirmation.

Frantically, Christina scanned the area for her purse, desperate for her Sidekick II. It was nowhere. She ransacked her brain, trying to remember when she last held her Hysteric Glamour bag. But everything was foggy. "Shit!" she screamed. "Somebody stole my purse!"

"*Relax*," Carb said. "I saw one behind the bar just a while ago. It's probably yours." He led the way.

Christina followed him, her mind racing. The sight of the leopard-print army fatigue–patterned handbag flooded her with relief.

She dashed for it and fished out her mobile, scrolling through the missed calls and the text message from Max.

Then she halted, almost too terrified to learn the outcome. Was Shoshanna dead or alive? Finally, Christina conjured up the courage to make the call.

Max picked up on the first ring.

The moment Christina heard his voice, she knew the answer.

From: Mimi

How killer is the NYC party scene?

2:09 am 4/09/06

chapter three

Where and when did you last see her?" the uniformed police officer asked.

Dante's stomach was in a tight ball of knots. He *knew* something had gone very wrong and the terrible feeling only grew exponentially with each passing moment. "At a party not far from here. I'm pretty sure it was after midnight."

"What kind of party?"

Dante fought hard to harness his annoyance. "A friend of ours put it together. He called it 'Tar Beach.' It was a rooftop blowout. I don't know the exact address."

"Big crowd?"

"Maybe a hundred or so. It was hard to tell. People were coming and going."

"Hey, Curran," another officer said as he approached. "Here's the chick we're looking for." In his hand was a magazine folded back to a page featuring celebrities in swimwear. Vanity St. John was shown cavorting around South Beach in a bikini. "Somebody had this at the front desk."

Curran glanced at the photo, then back to the other officer. There was a silent exchange between the two men that translated, "She's hot, man. I'd nail her." Typical guy shit. "Is she your girlfriend?"

Dante hesitated. "We're friends."

Curran searched Dante's face for greater meaning. "Friends with benefits?"

Dante glared at him. "Are you a real cop? Because this sounds like a Q and A I'd have with some dude over a beer."

The other officer snorted his laughter, then walked away muttering, "Mouthy little punk, isn't he?"

But Curran stayed put. He gave Dante a withering stare. "I'll ask the questions, kid. If you're sleeping with this girl, then more power to you. I'm not impressed. I'm not jealous, either. I'm just trying to get a solid read on the situation. You see, where I come from, a guy wouldn't let a 'friend' who looks like that leave a party and go back to her hotel room alone. Did the two of you have a fight?"

Dante sighed his frustration. "Does it matter?"

"I'll decide what information matters."

Dante sank down onto the bed and covered his face with his hands, feeling like precious time was being pissed away. "Yes, we had a fight."

"About what?"

"I couldn't tell you," Dante mumbled.

"What's that?"

This time Dante shouted his answer. "I couldn't tell you!"

"Why not?"

"Have you ever argued with a drunk girl?" Dante challenged.

Curran gave a rueful nod as if to concede the point.

"We had a fight at the party," Dante explained. "She left. I wasn't that far behind her—twenty minutes, a half hour at the most. I came straight to this room. The door was ajar, so I stepped inside. I found the place trashed just like it is now. That's when I called hotel security. And then I discovered that."

Dante pointed to the open bathroom. From his position on the edge of the bed, the message on the mirror was clearly visible.

A DIRTY BITCH WUZ HERE

Just seeing it again made Dante's body shudder.

Curran gave the blood graffiti a quick glance. "Any idea who might write something like that about your friend?"

Dante shook his head.

Curran's partner shuffled back and reentered the conversation. "Turns out this Vanity St. John is the same girl who had a sex video all over the Internet a few months ago. She also tried to off herself in Miami by ramming a brand-new Mercedes into a fuel tanker."

Curran studied Dante carefully. "Maybe she's an attention junkie. Any chance that she wrote those words on the mirror herself?"

Dante rose to his feet, stunned and more than a little angry now. "No way."

"Hey," Curran's partner put in, "stranger things have happened. Remember the runaway bride? That whack job hacked off her hair and faked a kidnapping."

"She didn't stage this!" Dante insisted.

"The staff on duty at the front desk saw her return to the hotel but didn't see her leave," Curran said in a tone so reasonable as to be patronizing. "Maybe she's with another friend in the hotel."

Curran's partner finger combed his goatee with a sigh. "This must be the night for famous young girls in trouble."

Curran gave him a curious glance. "How do you figure?"

"Didn't you hear? Max Biaggi's teenage daughter OD'd at some party."

The news hit Dante like a shock to the solar plexus. He just stood there, unable to think, to move, to breathe.

"You take a mortal man/And put him in control/Watch him become a god/Watch people's heads a' roll . . ."

The Megadeth track thrashed violently from the bookshelf stereo as Vanity lay there, every limb stretched to the limit and tightly bound, the Sony Handycam capturing every moment.

He stood over her, filming her stark mad fear, as if he were the director of the sickest reality show on earth.

"Please untie me," Vanity begged. "The ropes hurt."

In answer, he zoomed in for a close-up of her tear-stained face, a twisted smile curling his lips. "Pain is good drama."

Vanity fought for calm, struggling to piece together the events that had brought her to this point. Vividly, she remembered needing to leave Tar Beach, to get away from Dante. She had gone back to the hotel, where the asshole bartender at Wetbar refused to serve her a drink. There was a hostile exchange of words, and then she returned to her room.

After that, the memories seemed to just fade into oblivion . . . wait . . . she recalled something else now. An irritating episode at the door with her key card. She made a dozen or so attempts, but just couldn't get it to swipe properly. Of course, being wasted didn't help the situation. Finally, she conquered the task. The blinking green light above the knob had been her reward. All Vanity wanted to do was sleep. She pushed open the door.

And then someone had crashed into her body from behind, simultaneously forcing her inside the suite and covering her mouth with a foul-smelling handkerchief, at which point everything turned to black . . . until she woke up . . . here.

Different room. Same hotel. And the prisoner of Jayson "J.J." James.

He looked awful, like a man who had aged years within months. There had been a dramatic weight loss, a once-athletic body now gaunt and wiry. Even more alarming was the condition of his skin—rough, patchy, far and away from the sun-kissed surfer dude perfection of his Gap model days.

Their sordid history spiraled through Vanity's mind. A hot minute ago, J.J. was a second-tier male model with an appetite for drugs and partying. Vanity had met him on various shoots, seen him out at the major clubs. And more than once he had charmed her into a night that she would regret the next morning.

The most regrettable of all had been the Surfcomber incident. That's when J.J. set up a hidden camera to film their bedroom action. Learning about it had pushed Vanity to the edge, resulting in a deliberate car crash that left her unable to walk for months.

At first, Max had cut a deal with J.J. to bury the footage. But J.J. kept a copy and months later began selling the video as a pay-for-play download. Vanity's father had dispatched his attorneys to annihilate not only J.J., but also any website or Internet service offering the X-rated content. Though the legal maneuvering worked, the damage had already been done. So many had seen the tape and could still find it through clandestine channels.

"J.J., please . . . don't do this to me," Vanity cried out desperately.

" 'Don't do this to me.' " His voice was hoarse and mocking. "You're the one who's doing it. You put your daddy and his lawyers on my ass. They're watching me."

Vanity shook her head in disbelief. "What are you talking about?"

"They tapped my cellphone. They want to kill me."

She watched him stalk over to the mirrored hutch littered with crushed beer cans, garbage, and drug paraphernalia. His own four-hundred-dollar-a-night crack den.

J.J. grabbed a glass pipe and set it ablaze, making the tiny, fast-burning rock disappear as he expertly inhaled the smoke directly into his lungs.

Within a few seconds his eyes dilated, and he began to preen around the room, turning the camera on himself in a disturbing show of exhilaration and omnipotence.

Five minutes later he crashed, suddenly withdrawn and depressed. He rambled nonsensically, about the WB/UPN network merger ruining his shot at television stardom and about fashion editors conspiring to end his modeling career.

Vanity's fear intensified. Drugs had been part of her world since she was thirteen. Marijuana, pills, cocaine, crystal meth, heroin, ecstasy. The whole gamut was always available at parties, in VIP club rooms, from older friends, on photo shoots. She had seen every illegal substance be consumed by casual users and addicts alike.

But Vanity had never witnessed a true junkie up close, and that's exactly what J.J. had become. A total crackhead. And completely unpredictable. The sight was at once frightening and pathetic.

J.J. stepped back to the hutch, searching frantically for another white rock. He found a small pebble and proceeded to go through the motions again. Lighting the hot pipe . . . inhaling the sweet smoke . . . waiting for the quick high.

The telephone jangled, its subdued electronic ring barely competing with the relentless growl of Megadeth.

At first, J.J. merely stared, as if fascinated by the flashing light. But then he broke the trance and stepped over to the desk. "Hello . . . okay . . ." He hung up. "Somebody's complaining about the music."

Vanity quickly envisioned a strategy that might get someone to the room. And with J.J. halfway through the high of his last hit, the plan just might work. "Fuck them!" she screamed. "This is your room! Turn it up!"

His crazy eyes widened at the suggestion. "Yeah, you're right. *Fuck* them!"

Vanity's heart beat wildly inside her chest as she watched J.J. twist up the volume until the walls vibrated with the sonic assault of "Symphony of Destruction."

Suddenly, he stopped and zeroed in on her with a strange look, his face turning dark. "It's your dad's lawyers again! When are they going to leave me alone?"

Vanity watched in horror as J.J. produced a hunting knife with a gut hook and serrated edge. "I'll make them disappear. Untie me. Give me a chance to call my father. It'll be done. I promise." She tried to stare deep into his eyes, to reach him in some way.

J.J. scratched his arm with the knife, instantly drawing blood. But if he noticed the cut at all, it didn't register. That's how far gone he was.

Vanity struggled to wrench free from the tight knots. Her wrists were raw and bleeding from the rope burns, the pain so intense that it felt like her skin was being ripped all the way down to exposed bone. But the effort was futile.

Now J.J. stood over her and raised the knife.

Vanity's eyes focused on the steel blade.

"As long as Daddy's dirty bitch is alive, he's going to protect her," J.J. said.

And then his arm plunged down.

From: Max

My sister's in a coma. If she dies, so do you.

2:31 am 4/09/06

chapter four

max had never been so serious about anything in his life. If Shoshanna didn't pull through, then he stood ready to kill Vlad Singer.

The little bastard was famous for his chemistry skills in creating new and potent club drugs. Seeing the punk chatting up Sho at Tar Beach had filled Max with a worst-case fear. And right now he was living it.

Nobody had seen or heard from the MIT lab rat since Shoshanna collapsed. Max was calling everyone he knew—and even those that he didn't—following up on any lead, no matter how vague, desperately trying to locate him. Vlad was the only son of a bitch who knew the name and chemistry of the drug that had Sho fighting for her life.

Max sat in the hospital, a tight grip on his Sidekick II. He was practically willing the device to vibrate. Deep down, he yearned for a connection. Shit. *Any* voice would do right now. That included his father's.

Max hated waiting. *For anything.* It sucked. Especially for a guy who spent his entire life making other people wait. But there was a first time for everything. So this must be karma kicking Max Biaggi Jr. in the ass.

His Sidekick II rumbled. He glanced down to see DANTE CALLING on the screen. God, it seemed like their stupid argument at Tar Beach had happened weeks ago, yet it was only a few hours old. "Hey, man." Max's voice quivered.

"Dude, I just heard what went down. Where are you?"

"NYU Medical Center. Sho's in a coma."

Dante breathed a sigh of tempered relief. "Jesus, the cop said she OD'd. I thought she was dead."

Max choked up, rolling his body inward to control the convulsive sobs.

"Dude, she's going to pull out of this," Dante assured him. "Sho's a tough little girl."

"It's all my fault. I shouldn't have let her come to New York with me."

"Don't do this to yourself, man. You're not to blame."

Max heard the voice of his mother hiss inside his mind.

Where were you when your sister was doing drugs? Chasing some slut?

"I should've had that shitdick thrown out when I first saw him. I knew Vlad Singer was trouble. I *knew* it!"

"Sho's probably still alive because you *didn't* throw him out," Dante countered. "Think about it, man. She would've followed his ass straight out the door just to prove a point. He would've given her the same drugs, too. Only that punk probably would've freaked and just left her somewhere. But you were there, dude. You knew what to do. You saved her life."

Max allowed the words of support to sink in. It felt so good to hear them. After a few beats of silence, he finally spoke. "For now maybe."

"Mark my words. It won't be long before Sho's talking so much shit that you'll wish she was back in a coma."

Max laughed a little. "Thanks, man. I needed this. You know, for a maid's kid, you're not so bad."

Dante chuckled. "And as far as trust-fund twats go, I've met worse dudes than you."

Max cracked a smile. "This conversation is beginning to sound gay."

"Then let's just get it over with," Dante teased. "If you say 'I love you' first, I'll say it back."

"We're in New York," Max cracked. "Not on Brokeback Mountain. Hey, is Vanity with you?" A memory flashed. "Hold up—didn't you send me a text about trying to find her?"

Dante hesitated. "She's MIA right now. But as soon as I connect with her, we'll come to the hospital. Don't worry about it. You just hang in there."

Max started to reply, then stopped once he saw Dr. Elizabeth Tang walking toward him. "Okay, man," he murmured distantly, hanging up.

"Your sister's condition has improved," Dr. Tang announced crisply and without preamble. "She's out of the coma and in recovery now."

Max's heart soared. Overcome with emotion, he closed his eyes, as if to seal in the most critical moment of his life so far. *Sho was okay.*

"I've seen cases like this before," Dr. Tang went on. "There's not much hope that the toxicology screen will tell us anything about the actual substance and dosage that caused her to end up here." She paused a beat to level a harsh look. "Club drugs are insidious that way."

"I don't know what she took," Max said, feeling judged and under attack. "If I did, don't you think I'd come clean? She's my sister."

"And you're lucky to be using the present tense when you talk about her," Dr. Tang admonished.

"What's your problem with me?" Max asked hotly. "I realize how serious this is, but I'm not responsible for it."

Dr. Tang stared back impassively. "Maybe I've just seen too many cases like this—young and smart rich kids playing Russian roulette with drugs they know nothing about. A trip to the emergency room should be a final warning, but for most of you, it's nothing more than an interruption of the party."

"Don't hold it in, Doc. Tell me how you really feel."

"I think I just did," Dr. Tang shot back. "The plot for teenagers like you is pretty easy to follow." One beat. "Sort of like your father's dumb movies. I hope you approach this as a wake-up call." She started to walk away.

"When can I see her?" Max called out.

Dr. Tang halted. "We're getting her started on fluids for an electrolyte imbalance. It won't be much longer. One of the nurses will let you know when it's time." And then she was gone.

Max stood there, replaying the exchange, wondering if the bitch doctor might be right. At the end of the day, would he treat this as a real life lesson . . . or just another dodged bullet?

Pippa sat on the Boeing 737 as it made the descent into Miami, trying to think of just one man in her life who hadn't—eventually—revealed himself to be a lying, cheating shitbag.

Drummond Keith, her very own father, with his closeted homosexuality, drug addictions, and incompetent business dealings hardly qualified as an exception.

The same could be said for Hugh Somerset, father of Annabelle, her best mate back in London. On a weekend sleepover, Pippa once caught him peeking at her while she bathed. And even after she screamed upon discovering him, the bloody perv didn't stop polishing his knob. Vile!

Tonight she could add Max Biaggi to the list. And Vinnie Rossetti, too. The manager of Cheetah cozied up to her at the club, calling her his "favorite girl" and his "golden pussy." Then he turned around and pimped her out on a rape date like some street hooker. Low-rent mobster pig!

Pippa stewed in a minicauldron of hurt and rage. *Men.* They thought they could just use her for their own selfish needs. But now maybe it was Pippa's turn to use *them.*

Throughout her life, men had conditioned Pippa to think of herself in second-class terms. She had waited around for any sign that her daddy loved her. She had kept the dirty secret of her best friend's father. She had followed Vinnie's instructions to the letter, aiming to please, coveting the favorite-girl slot. And she had allowed Max Biaggi to fool her into thinking that tonight was something more than it was.

But it was time for a new order. Why be used when she could be the user? Why be the victim when she could be the victor? A plan began to percolate in her mind. It would take balls of steel to pull off, but she had them. Tonight a man had fucked with Pippa Keith for the last time. And she was going to make Max Biaggi pay the symbolic price for every bastard who had ever wronged her.

He slumped in the leather chair opposite her, avoiding eye contact, knocking back another hard drink, looking generally pissed off.

Pippa studied him intently. Bit by bit, she could feel her heart calcify as she put the ugly facts together.

She had built him up as this larger-than-life, perfect creature—an iconic big-screen action hero, a misunderstood father, a truly amazing man. And yet the whole time she was nothing more than a whore to him.

The pathetic fantasy had been constructed in her wounded little-girl mind. He was the prince. She was the princess. He would save her from the burning castle, marry her, and together they would live out the ultimate Hollywood dream. But the cold reality was that even a kiss on the lips was out of the question. That's how much he disrespected her.

Pippa's mind raced with the dark revenge fantasy, summing it up, sorting it out. Max Biaggi probably expected her to slink away like a stupid, weak-willed disposable slut, the kind of girl so beaten down emotionally and spiritually that she believed her only real value was her body. Too bad the bastard was about to be *very* disappointed.

"I want a trust fund," Pippa announced. Her tone was defiant and matter-of-fact.

"Oh yeah? Well, I want an Oscar. Good luck to both of us." Max Biaggi sneered, draining the last swallow of dark liquor from his crystal highballer. He poured another.

"I'm serious."

"So am I." He didn't bother to look in her direction.

Pippa reflected on Max Junior and all of his flashy material possessions, not to mention the eight-figure nest egg that would help secure any future that he chose to seek out. "As I understand it, your son's trust stands at fifty-one-point-two million."

Max Biaggi glanced up, alarmed by her intimate knowledge of the family numbers.

Pippa challenged him with her gaze. "I'm only asking for a fraction of that . . . say . . . one million."

He raised his glass, giving her a fuck-you grin. "Sure, baby, sure. I'll put a check in the mail."

The superjet's wheels touched down on the tarmac, and Pippa waited for the plane to glide to a smooth stop before unfastening her seat belt and leaning forward to deliver the hammer blow. "Underestimating how serious I am could be very hazardous to your image. It might even impact future career earnings. So all things considered, I'd say you're getting off pretty cheap." She stood up.

Max Biaggi lurched to his feet, grabbed her upper arm,

and squeezed so tight that she cried out in agony. "Do you actually think you can blackmail me, bitch?"

Pippa twisted out of his grasp and beamed back a look of daring comeuppance. "Don't be so negative. Approach it as a business arrangement—my confidentiality for your generosity."

"You'll be lucky to get a ride back to the club."

Pippa iced him down with a bring-it-on glare. She wasn't afraid anymore. If anything, he would be wise to fear her now. And her body language communicated this loud and clear. "I don't mind walking. Besides, it'll make a damn good story when I sit down for an interview with Diane Sawyer."

Max Biaggi narrowed his eyes, silently sizing her up.

Pippa gave him a smug look. "Or maybe it'll be Oprah. She loves victims. And when I sink my teeth into a role, I can play it to the hilt. Ask your son. He was there when I brought the house down in *Sweet Charity*."

"I'm not going to let some teenage whore extort me!"

"Careful, dear," Pippa trilled in a singsong voice. "This isn't a negotiation. It's an offer. And if you reject it, the next deal on the table might be for two million."

Max Biaggi's face turned red with fury, and his dark eyes practically bulged from their sockets.

The flight attendant who'd been banished to the service cabin upon takeoff emerged to assist them with deplaning.

"This must be so frustrating for a bloke like you," Pippa whispered teasingly. "Such an expensive piece of ass. And you didn't even get the chance to enjoy it." She slipped past him, acknowledging the attendant and breathing in the gorgeous Miami night/morning as she carefully negotiated the stairs in her nosebleed Manolos.

The same white limousine and driver were waiting on the runway.

Max Biaggi came bounding down and intercepted her on the last step. "Do you really think you can take me on?" He was mere inches from her face, doing his best menacing rich-man act.

"You had a plan for how things would go tonight, but you're still horny and about to be a million dollars poorer. I'm not only taking you on, Mr. Movie Star, I'm kicking your ass."

"Do you have any idea what I could do to you?"

"You've already done it," Pippa replied. "That's why you're going to pay me the million." One beat. "Not a single word of this to Vinnie. As far as he's concerned, I'm still of legal age, and you had a great time." She started for the limousine, then stopped and spun around. "I'm going home to take time- and date-stamped photographs of my bruises, and then I'm going to write in my journal about everything you said and did to me so that detail and nuance is on my side. Have your lawyer draw up a contract formalizing our agreement. I'll be hiring my own attorney to protect my interests and manage the trust."

Max Biaggi's lips parted in surprise. The impression lingered that the mind of a teenage girl with a fake ID wasn't supposed to work with such ball-crunching shrewdness.

"By the way," Pippa added, "I don't think the limo is big enough for both of us. Have the driver take me to my car at the club. He can come back for you later." With that, she slipped into the cabin and waited to be whisked away from the private airstrip.

She thought about Vinnie on the drive to Cheetah. He was so working class, possessing all the sophistication of an ape, a total chav for sure. But unlike Max Biaggi, who feared negative media headlines like paranoid schizophrenics feared alien abductions, Vinnie Rossetti fancied himself a Gold Coast Tony Soprano. Basically, *nothing* scared the goomba. He was tough guy personified.

For weeks, rumors had been swirling among dancers at the club about Ashley, Vinnie's former number one stage girl who had left him to strip at Scores. She openly recruited other Cheetah girls to do the same until she ended up in the hospital with beating injuries so brutal that she would be lucky to ever dance again. The official story was an attempted carjacking, but everybody knew that Vinnie had arranged the attack.

Pippa knew the smart way to handle Vinnie. And that

was very carefully. If he ever discovered that she was underage and jeopardizing the doors to the club staying open . . . well, God, she didn't even want to ponder the outcome.

Suddenly, Pippa felt a knot of emotion in her throat. Tears sprang to her eyes. She longed to reach out for someone. Instantly, Max popped into mind. Her darling Max. So comforting in his funny, naughty way. Pippa experienced a stab of sadness as she came to grips with the fact that nothing would ever be the same between them.

That face, those eyes. Max was the mirror image of his father. How could she ever look at him and not be reminded of this horrible night? No, it was best to pull away. For her sake. And for his, too. If Max ever found out about . . . God, Pippa didn't even want to ponder that.

All she could think about was leaving Miami. Everything had gone so wrong. She had to get out. Somewhere else. Anywhere else. Pippa wanted nothing more than to quit stripping, too. But for now, at least, it was a necessary evil. She needed every bit of cash she could get her hands on. And who knew how long it might take to finalize the trust?

The limousine coasted to a stop, and the driver killed the engine, then swung around to open the rear passenger door.

Pippa stepped out to find herself in Cheetah's dingy

rear parking lot. There was her junkyard Chevrolet and next to it a gleaming white Infiniti Q45 . . . Hellcat's car.

The mean bitch leaned against the luxury sedan, smoking a cigarette and playing with the catch and release of her switchblade.

Pippa said her good-byes to the driver, located her keys, and made a beeline for her vehicle.

"Well, well, if it isn't Cinderella," Hellcat taunted. "How was the ball?"

Pippa worked hard to ignore her. The events of the night had left her shell-shocked. The last thing she needed was a run-in with Hellcat.

"So did the glass slipper fit?"

Pippa pretended not to hear, determined to simply get in her car and drive away.

The key was just about to unlock the door when Hellcat flicked away her hand. "I'm talking to you, bitch."

Pippa felt a surge of unstoppable, all-powerful rage. Her moves were swift and certain, yet dangerously out of control. She had the advantage of surprise, and the melee ended with Hellcat sprawled on the hood of the Infiniti and the business end of the switchblade millimeters from her throat.

"Now *I'm* talking," Pippa hissed, moving the weapon even closer to skin and vein, simultaneously astonished and empowered by her own propensity for violence. "You struck a nerve. I've been called a bitch one too many times tonight."

Hellcat swallowed hard.

"I don't know what your problem is with me," Pippa went on. "Maybe it's because I'm young and lush, and you're an old cow. Maybe it's because that crappy stage inside is as good as it gets for you, and I've got bigger things in life waiting for me. It doesn't matter, though, because your problem ends tonight. I suggest you find a way to cope. See a therapist. Buy a self-help book. Try yoga. But leave me alone!"

Pippa snapped the blade closed and tossed it across the parking lot. Then she got in her car and drove away, feeling an eerie, detached sense of calm.

Her Nokia sang to life to the music of "I'm in Love (wit a Stripper)" by T-Pain and Mike Jones. It was Max's dedicated ring tone. Reluctantly, she picked up.

He seemed grateful to hear her voice, and as he relayed the story of Shoshanna's overdose and near death, Max lost control of his emotions more than once, crying openly, telling her how much he missed her, needed her, and loved her.

But his sentiments didn't penetrate her numbness. Pippa just concentrated on the road and listened to him ramble on, realizing that the night had changed her, almost turned her into a different girl altogether. Because Max, her best mate, was pouring out his heart, and Pippa felt absolutely nothing.

She was as cold as ice.

From: Mom

I heard about Max's sister on CNN. I want you home
on the next plane and away from that group.

3:09 am 4/09/06

chapter five

"I've got a source that says she died on the table, and they brought her back to life," one freelance photographer said.

"I hear she was only in a light coma, but is out of it now and doing fine," another shutterbug replied.

A female news reporter checked her makeup with a jeweled compact. "Are we sure it's a drug thing? Maybe one of her implants sprung a leak." She chortled. "Can you believe that was her father's idea of a birthday gift for turning fifteen?" Staring in the direction of First Avenue, she huffed impatiently. "I'm paying back a fortune in journalism school loans to wait around for this shit. I should be the one in there suffering from an overdose."

The first photographer laughed, taking a final swig of Red Bull and crushing the can.

"If you think that's funny, you should see my pay stub," she grumbled. "I can't earn side money off these freaks. How much do you guys stand to make for a shot tonight anyway?"

"Max Biaggi alone usually fetches around a thousand," the second photographer offered. "But this will be him rushing inside the hospital to see about his dying daughter. Should easily clear twenty-five grand."

Christina struggled to get through the cluster of bodies blocking the hospital entrance. The mercenary zeal of the tabloid media disgusted her. Nothing was sacred anymore.

Carb led the way, aggressively pushing toward the door until they were safely inside. "You okay?"

Christina nodded, stunned that he had insisted on accompanying her to NYU Medical Center without so much as a pause to find clean clothes.

He remained shirtless in his vomit-soiled jeans, yet he still looked good enough to eat. And this aesthetic appreciation was from a lesbian.

Christina smiled. "You don't have to stay, Carb. I promise not to jump off the roof of this building." She held up her Sidekick II as evidence. "And I say this *after* reading the most recent text from my mother."

"At least allow me to transfer you to the custody of a friend before I take off," Carb said.

"I'm here to offer *him* support," Christina pointed out.

"Oh yeah? That sounds like the blind leading the blind."

She halted, slightly offended. "I'm not crazy, you know."

"I'll take your word on that. Because I've only known you to be falling-down drunk, dangling from the roof of a building by a string of Christmas lights, or throwing up things that you ate two years ago."

"If you only knew how boring I really was," Christina said softly.

Carb grinned. "We're a half hour into this new friendship, and you're anything but boring."

She laughed.

"It should be this way," Carb said, taking off fast, his long legs in full stride.

Christina struggled to keep in step.

"Jap!" The familiar voice carried the familiar, much-hated nickname.

Christina glanced up to see Max rushing in her direction, looking exhausted, relieved, and desperate for company.

When he reached her, his embrace was all-consuming. "Sho's resting now, but I just saw her a few minutes ago." He drew back and took both of her hands in his. "Jesus, I was so scared, Jap. She came close to . . . shit, I can't even say it. But she's okay now. The doctor just wants to keep her here for the next several hours. You know, for observation."

Christina squeezed his hands. "It's a lucky night."

Max nodded, cutting his eyes over to Carb. "Who's the Chippendales dancer?"

Christina smiled and made the necessary introduction. "He's a new friend," she told Max. "A lifesaver, in fact."

"I should go," Carb said.

"Yeah," Max agreed, a little too quickly. "Maybe find a shirt or something."

Christina beamed a secret look to Carb, an apology in her eyes.

He grinned, silently assuring her that it was no big deal. "Take care of yourself. I'm heading out." Carb started to walk away.

"Wait!" Christina called out. "How do I get in touch with you?"

"You'll figure it out one day." And then Carb Duffy was gone.

Regretfully, Christina watched him disappear, then turned back to give Max a scolding glare. "*Find a shirt?*"

Max shrugged, impervious to any wrongdoing. "Hey, it needed to be said."

Christina rolled her eyes. "The media wagons are circling. There's a group out front waiting for your dad to arrive."

A dark expression clouded Max's face. "The son of a

bitch doesn't even know about this yet. He won't answer his phone."

"He'll know soon enough. My mom saw it on CNN. She wants me home on the next plane."

Max shook his head in disgust. "Well, at least she gives a shit."

"That's debatable," Christina murmured.

"Take it from me," he argued gently. "At times like these, an overbearing parent would be nice."

Christina said nothing. Max had no idea what she faced upon return to Miami. A mother who would rather see her dead than gay. Two weeks at Salvation Pointe being brainwashed by Jesus freaks.

Given the choice, Christina would prefer the parent who didn't give a damn. She considered confessing all to Max, then thought better of it. Right now he had his own problem with Shoshanna. This was hers to deal with. Besides, he would never understand what if felt like to be under the suffocating rule of a controlling parent.

Christina glanced around. "Where is everybody?"

"I talked to Dante a few minutes ago," Max said. "He's trying to find Vanity." He sighed, holding up his Sidekick. "Then I got through to Pippa and broke down like a blubbering idiot. She didn't have much to say, either. Probably thinks I'm a whiny little bitch." He wiped his eyes and looked close to tears again.

Christina touched his arm. "I'm sure she was taken

aback. Everybody counts on you for a laugh, Max. You're the comic relief. It's hard to watch that person fall apart."

"I don't know. I can't figure her out anymore." He shrugged and grinned at Christina. "I'm glad you're here, though." And then he pulled her in for an embrace.

Christina hugged him tightly, needing it just as much. "Shoshanna's okay," she whispered. "Everything's going to be okay."

For a long second, he became very still. "Ugh . . . you smell like puke, Jap."

"Shut up and cry, Max."

"New York's a big city—"

"Is it?" Dante cut in savagely. "Didn't know that. Thanks for the geography lesson, Sipowicz."

Curran was already pissed. Now he was more pissed. "Listen, smart-ass, if we could put dedicated man hours on every drunk girl who gets in a fight with her boyfriend and disappears for a few hours, then that would mean we were living in Candyland."

Dante was fuming.

"Just relax and give this some time," Curran went on. "Most of these things sort themselves out. We've talked to everyone on duty. Nobody saw her leave the hotel. We have every reason to believe she's still on the property."

"If I have to go room to room and knock on every

goddamn door of this hotel, then that's what I'll do!"

"Try knocking on just one door." As Curran painted the threat, his cheeks turned red. "You'll be taking a ride with me to the precinct. Bet on it."

Dante experienced a helpless anxiety. There was no time to wait. The horrible feeling lanced in his gut told him so. He pointed an accusing finger at Curran. "Dude, if anything happens to her . . . it's going to mean your badge. I'll tell this story to anybody who'll listen, and you'll be lucky to get a gig as a night watch rent-a-cop."

Curran shook his head dismissively. "Why don't you get some sleep, tough guy? Could be that this girl's just hiding from *you*."

The fight was out of Dante. This NYPD loser was a complete waste of time. He tried to think about his next move, wondering if he should call Simon St. John, Vanity's father. Then he vaguely noticed the hotel's assistant manager taking a call on his Bluetooth earpiece.

"Yes . . . I'll head over there right now . . . eight thirteen . . . got it . . . Crystal, who's registered to that room?"

Dante rubbed his tired, bloodshot eyes.

"Jayson James . . . okay . . . comp one night's charges to the guest who called in the complaints."

Dante spun around to face the manager. A hot current of certainty shocked his body. It was electric. "He's got her."

"Who's got her?" Curran asked.

"Jayson James," Dante said. "He's the guy responsible for the Internet sex tape. Vanity's father buried him in lawsuits."

"So where do we find this Jayson James?"

Dante ignored Curran and zeroed in on the manager. "Room eight thirteen, right?"

"That call isn't related to this matter. It's just a loud music com—"

Dante vaulted toward the door, praying to God that he wouldn't be too late.

The will to scream had evaporated from Vanity's psyche. This would be the end. Right here. Right now.

A bloody finale.

J.J.'s knife swooped down again, his face a mask of unspeakable rage and drug-ravaged disconnect.

Vanity braced herself for the impact, but once more J.J. had shifted aim at the last possible moment, gutting the mattress mere inches from her body.

The torture was unbearable. On some level she just wanted him to stab her straight through the heart and get it over with.

But J.J. seemed to have enough presence of mind to realize this, so he gleefully prolonged the inevitable kill.

Megadeth's "Symphony of Destruction" continued to

roar inside the room. The track was locked in repeat mode. It played over and over again.

Vanity felt her mind shutting down. Facing her own mortality was too much to endure. Especially now. There were so many regrets gnawing away at her soul as she lay here, sweating out the seconds until she was butchered.

She would die not being at peace with anyone in her personal orbit. The connection to her mother was almost nonexistent, and the rift with her father seemed to grow wider each day.

Almost every primary relationship in Vanity's life had either deteriorated or been left in a fractured mess. Her dealings with Max were superficial at best. Pippa had all but disappeared from her life. After tonight's drunken kiss, Christina would probably never speak to her again. And Dante certainly had no reason to, either. So maybe she deserved to go out like this.

But she wanted another chance. To prove her value as a friend. To change her life. To make better choices. Oh God . . . leaving everyone . . . the way things were . . . that saddened Vanity more than the idea of dying itself.

J.J.'s eyes took on a strange expression, as if the joy for cheap scare thrills had given way to a lust for blood and murder.

He raised the knife. "Any last words, dirty bitch?"

Vanity stared into the face of her killer and felt nothing. What escaped from her lips was a sad, broken, vacant whisper. "Just do it."

Bam! Bam! Bam!

J.J. froze, startled by the ferocious pounding on the door. "They're here." He spoke in a crazy, paranoid voice.

"Mr. James, this is the police." The male voice rang out with authority. "I'm asking you to open the door. If you fail to do so, we will be coming inside on our own."

"It's not the police. It's your father's lawyers. They're here to take everything away from me. They want it all." J.J. talked in a rapid clip as he paced the limits of the room.

Vanity's gaze tracked the door with laser intensity.

"Mr. James?" It sounded like the policeman's final warning.

She turned to J.J. and knew instantly that he stood ready to break. There was an insane panic in his eyes that chilled her. "It's not the lawyers," Vanity told him. "They're in Miami. We're in New York."

For several long seconds, J.J. just stared at her. "Liar," he finally said.

The suite door burst open.

J.J. lunged without warning. He screamed like a wild beast. And he stabbed at Vanity with sadistic abandon.

The knife's tip narrowly missed her shoulder, but the blade sliced into her upper arm. Blood gushed.

Vanity was too shocked to scream or feel any pain.

And then she saw him . . . Dante . . . exploding inside the room, colliding with J.J. in a full-on body tackle that sent both of them crashing down to the floor.

Seconds after that, it was over.

Two officers subdued J.J.

The hotel manager called for an ambulance.

One of the officers cut her free.

Dante ripped a sheet to tourniquet the stab wound, inspecting her body for other injuries. "I don't think he got you anyplace else."

But she just lay there, immobile, unable to answer.

"Vanity!" Dante cried. His warm hands cradled her face. "Are you with me?"

Finally, she grinned, ever so faintly.

And then he pulled her in for an embrace so loving and so tender that Vanity could only feel her heart swell with gratitude—for being alive.

"Yes, Dante . . . I'm with you."

"Wait a minute. I'm the firstborn of a freaking action star. So how does this welfare case manage to swoop in and play the hero?" Max asked.

"Because there was a fight scene, bitch," Dante said. "And you refuse to do your own stunts."

Everybody laughed.

Dante, Max, and Christina were gathered around Vanity's hospital bed at New York University Medical Center. Though tired, she felt surprisingly good. The stab wound had been treated and dressed, and the emergency room intern had promised an early morning release.

Attentively, Dante brushed a tendril of hair from her forehead with his hand.

Vanity smiled at him as she took in more ice shavings.

Max continued on. "Jap is the one we should really be feeling sorry for."

Christina gave him an amused look. "And why's that?"

"Well, think about it. Sho got media coverage. Vanity's got the press chasing her like jackals. Then there's you, hanging upside down off the side of a building by a string of Christmas lights . . . and you can't get so much as a mention in a neighborhood newsletter."

"Max!" Vanity protested, smiling as she said it. He could be so hilariously awful.

"Well, I prefer it that way!" Christina insisted with good humor.

Max hooked an arm around Christina's waist and pulled her in close, kissing her on the side of the head. "I know you do, Jap."

Vanity watched them, feeling the tiniest pang of jealousy. She and Max would always have a strong connection. Their history tracked as far back as grade school. But day to day, their reliance on each other had faded. At one point, Pippa had become his anointed "best girl pal." Now Christina seemed to be filling the slot.

"How's Shoshanna?" Vanity asked.

Max's smile dimmed. "Probably wishing she was still in a coma. She's on her way back to Miami with Dad. But Sho could be worse than miserable. She could be in a body bag."

There was a tense silence.

Vanity threaded her fingers through Dante's hand.

He responded by clasping tight, his thumb caressing the top of her hand.

"Sho's a lucky girl," Vanity said earnestly. "So is Christina. And so am I. We're all lucky. To be here. To have one another." She reached for Christina.

Christina accepted the gesture and, in kind, slipped her hand into Max's.

To complete the circle, Max reluctantly took hold of Dante's hand. "This is a little gay, but I'm not opposed to the occasional 'Kumbaya' moment."

In answer, Dante pulled Max's hand to his lips and kissed it with a loud smack. "I love you, man."

Vanity gave them a stern look. "Can you guys be serious for one minute?"

"Yes, of course," Max said through a smile. But the act of trying clearly made the task more difficult. Finally, he broke up, saying, "Dude, I want to make out with you so bad."

Dante lost it.

Vanity was beyond exasperated, turning helplessly to Christina. "It's, like, all of a sudden they're twelve!"

The subdued Latina merely shook her head. "*All of a sudden?*"

Dante leaned in to kiss Vanity's cheek. "Baby, I'm sorry. Okay, no more. It's out of my system. I'm good. Let's do this." He closed his eyes, refusing to look at Max.

Vanity regarded him. The impact of how handsome Dante was sometimes hit her unexpectedly. Feelings were burgeoning between them, strong romantic vibrations, and instead of trying to define it, she was content to just give in to them. The most incredible thing was that she was sober while doing it. A definite first.

"I'll start," Max said.

Vanity gave him a warning look.

"*Seriously.*" He cleared his throat. "I went through the scariest night of my life last night. But I didn't go through it alone. I don't think I could have."

Emotion got caught in Vanity's throat right away.

Max continued. "A piece of my heart has always been missing. I think we all have that in common. Maybe it's the parent who's left us. Maybe it's the parent who's still around but doesn't see us. I don't know. All I can say is that I've always gone through life thinking that Sho was the only family that I had. Now I know that's not true anymore."

There was a brief silence.

"So . . . are you saying that I'm like a brother?" Dante asked.

Vanity looked at her oldest friend. The glint in his eyes told her that the sentimental Max had left the building.

"Yes, you're like a brother, you poor bastard. But that doesn't mean I'm putting you in the will."

Vanity laughed through her tears. She didn't let go of Dante's hand. She didn't let go of Christina's, either. She just held on to them, allowing the wonderful, connected feeling to sink in.

If only the moment could last . . .

From: Vanity

Exercise, tanning spa, and shopping.
Are you in for a total girl's day?

6:04 am 4/12/06

chapter six

Jennifer Lopez jogged past with her trainer, barely out of breath and looking fabulous.

"The first mile is always my hardest," Vanity said. "After that, I get into a zone, and the next four are easy."

"*Five* miles?" Christina huffed.

Vanity glanced backward. They were running her favorite South Beach route, from First to Fifteenth Street. Clarification: she was running it. Poor Christina was gasping for air and close to a total collapse. "Do you need to stop?"

Christina nodded gratefully, coming to a standstill. "Actually . . . I never . . . should've . . . started." Her breathing was ragged. "How do you . . . do this?"

Vanity walked toward her, grinning. "How do you *not* do it and stay so skinny?"

"It's my metabolism, I guess," Christina reasoned, still flushed. "I never gain weight."

"Lucky bitch. I hate you."

"To drag me out of bed for this? You must."

Vanity did a full-body stretch in her Stella McCartney for Adidas performance wear. "I tried to get Pippa to come, but she never responded to my text."

"Pippa who?" Christina asked rhetorically.

" 'Pippa who' is right. For all we know she could be back living in England."

They started to walk.

Vanity took in the scenery. Even though it had been months since Hurricane Wilma, many of the stairway-to-heaven skyscrapers still had boarded up, blown-out windows.

Christina was still recovering from the aborted run.

Vanity pushed her mango-flavored Propel into the girl's hand. "Here. Drink up before you dehydrate."

She guzzled half the bottle.

Vanity shook her head. "To have that body and be so out of shape. It's criminal."

Christina's cheeks blushed pink. And it had nothing to do with exhaustion.

"I'm sorry," Vanity said. "Was that a weird thing to say? I didn't mean—"

Christina waved off the apology. "No, don't be—"

"I just—"

"It's fine—"

"*Christina.*" Vanity's voice was firm but gentle. "We have to talk about what happened in New York. We have to clear the air between us."

Christina sighed. "Let's just forget that it happened."

"Can you forget it?" Vanity repossessed the Propel and took a generous gulp. "Can you forgive it?"

Christina shrugged. "You were drunk."

"I was mean."

"You were *drunk.*"

"I was disrespectful."

"Vanity, you don't have to do this. That night was insane. Given the chance, all of us would go back and live it differently."

"I just don't want you to think that I would ever intentionally mock your feelings. I was in a terrible head space that night."

"And you were *drunk,*" Christina said.

"Yes, I was. Believe it or not, I've been known to do some very stupid things in that condition."

"Well, let's just add that to the list and move on." A devilish smile crept onto Christina's lips. "Anyway, get over yourself. It wasn't that great of a kiss."

Vanity gasped. "Okay, you've been hanging around Max way too much. He's ruining you."

Christina laughed.

"And you're such a liar," Vanity accused lightly. "That was an awesome kiss, and you know it."

Now Christina drew in a shocked breath. "Oh, you totally need to get over yourself!" She laughed again, then tripped off to some distant place, appearing sad all of a sudden.

"What's wrong?" Vanity asked.

It took Christina a moment to answer. "Nothing. It's just . . . I'm going to miss times like these."

"I don't understand."

She hesitated. "You know, after we graduate."

"Me, too," Vanity murmured. But she had a gut feeling that Christina was holding back the real answer. "Have you decided about that art school in Savannah?"

"I got in," Christina said glumly. "For once being a female minority is a plus. The package they're offering is hard to turn down."

"So why don't you sound more excited?" Vanity asked.

Christina stared off into the distance. "I thought it was what I wanted. Now I'm not so sure." She paused a beat. "I'm feeling a little stronger. Maybe I should try to run again." She took off at an impressive clip.

Vanity caught up within a few strides, even though Christina was a million miles away . . .

*   *   *

One week later, Dante Medina was considering something much more dangerous than a street jog.

"Backwards," Max taunted. "I dare you."

"You *dare* me?" Dante laughed. "Does that line even work after the third grade?"

"Okay, if you don't do it, then you're a pussy."

"Oh, shit, it's *on* now, dude."

"Well, quit stalling, man. I'm waiting. The tourists are, too. Same goes for the fishermen. Give us a decent show."

Dante turned his back to the amazing sunset, balanced his feet on the edge of the South Pointe Pier, and sucked in a nervous breath, preparing to dive.

"You need to make at least two complete revolutions," Max said. "Otherwise, you're just a clumsy bitch falling backwards."

"Dude, shut up," Dante snapped. "I'm trying to concentrate. And since when are you a diving expert? You've done one cannonball from up here. And that barely made a splash."

"It's because I'm so lean."

"*Dude.* I mean it. Shut the fuck up. This is some reckless shit I'm about to try."

"All I'm saying is that if you want big splashes, bring a fat girl next time."

Dante gave him a withering look. "Okay, now I'm doing it just to get away from you."

And then he jumped up and out, arching his back, twisting and tucking on his way down, charged by the weightless feeling, pumped with adrenaline by the rocket speed as his body approached the water. Dante was three or four meters from breaking distance. Straightening his figure line, he tightened his muscles and smoothly entered the deep.

When he swam to the surface, a gaggle of tourists were clapping like seals.

"Not bad," Max shouted. "If I'm being honest, though, your feet could've been closer together!"

Dante shot up his middle finger. On principle. Then he ventured back, ignoring the NO DIVING warning signs and slipping past the chain-link fence, earning tipped hats and thumbs-ups from a few fishermen on the pier.

Upon reaching Max, Dante was wet and cold, but cocky as hell. "Your turn."

His smart-ass buddy grinned. "I don't have to do water tricks. I drive a Porsche."

Dante came *thisclose* to shoving him off the edge.

Max bent down to open the minicooler. "Heads-up, Mr. St. John."

Dante caught the cold bottle of Bud Light midair and twisted off the cap. "Thanks. You can't dive for shit, but you make a cute barmaid." He chugged the beer halfway down and played copycat to Max, dangling his legs off the pier, alternately gazing out at the ship channel action and the vastness of the ocean.

"Promise me something," Max said. His voice was soft, his tone serious.

"What?" Dante asked.

"Promise me you won't become Kevin Federline."

Dante elbowed him. "Asshole."

Max clutched his side and laughed. "I'm serious, man. I couldn't handle it if you went all K-Fed on me." One beat. "Or in your case, D-Med. And speaking of, what's up with your music? I haven't heard you say shit about it since that Speed Freak incident."

Dante relived the personal Waterloo. His idea to sample Henry Mancini's "Le Jazz-Hot" on a new song called "Le Hip-Hop" had been stolen by a lying son of a bitch named Juan Barba, recorded by Juan's younger brother, and then released on Alcatraz Records, the label operated by Vanity's father. And worse than the double cross was the fact that the track had become an all-out smash.

"I'm not feeling it," Dante mumbled.

"Well, you need to start feeling something," Max shot back. "Unless you intend to just hang around waiting for Vanity to give you milk money the rest of your life."

Dante felt the fire of a quickly lit anger. "Dude, Vanity hasn't given me a goddamn thing. And you're one to talk. All this bullshit about hating your father. Meanwhile, you're still nursing the trust-fund tit."

"You're absolutely right. I'm a total hypocrite. But I do drive a Porsche. Have I mentioned that?"

"Yeah, I think that's come up once or twice." Dante finished the Bud Light, scowling.

"Just don't lose sight of what you really want, man. That's all I'm saying. It's easy to get caught up in being Vanity's boyfriend. I've roamed that jungle, and I got lost in it, too. *Me*. So you don't stand a chance. I mean, think about it. You're just a maid's kid. And I'm Max Biaggi Jr."

Dante shook his head, pissed off but laughing anyway. "Sometimes I hate you, dude."

Unfazed, Max thundered on. "There's also the fact that you played superhero, which means you've got all this savior shit floating around in your head. Add some good sex to this list of ingredients, and you have a recipe for one very fucked-up Dante Medina." He punctuated his analysis by taking a sip of Bud Light and popping his lips on the bottle top.

"And let me tell you something about the music business, my friend." Max was on a roll, showing no signs of slowing down. "It's not an industry for pussies. Metaphorically speaking. If you actually have a pussy, that can be a plus. It's helped many a pop starlet get at least a hit single or two. But if you *are* a pussy, then that's not good at all. Okay, so Juan Barba stole your song idea. Life sucks, bitch. Get over it. Time for your next move. I mean, come on. You've got to have more than one song idea. Otherwise, I'm going to change your name to Baha Men. Remember them? They sang 'Who Let the Dogs Out.' Never heard from those fuckers again." Max laughed. "Or 'Macarena.' How about that name, you lazy one-hit wonder? Maybe you can tattoo *that* on your arm. Jesus!" Max let out an exasperated sigh and drank up.

Dante stared out at the water. "Are you done?"

"Yeah, that's all I've got. Pretty good, huh?"

Dante nodded. "I have to admit, the speech had its moments. I can't help but feel motivated."

Max's voice went up an octave. "Really? That's awesome."

"Of course, I still want to kick your ass."

"Well, you know what they say. You can take the biracial boy out of the barrio . . ."

Dante laughed. "Pass me another beer, asshole."

Max did so with a flourish. "Now don't sit there and think I'm living under the delusion that my side of the street is clean. After what happened with Sho in New York, I had to step back and reassess."

"And what'd you come up with?" Dante asked.

"The party-boy shit is in the past. I've got something else cooking."

Dante looked at him. "For real?"

Max nodded emphatically.

"No more big events?"

"Done with that."

"Poker games?"

"Over it."

Dante was genuinely intrigued. "So what's the deal?"

"Just keep next Saturday night open." His voice was cryptic, leaving Dante to wonder.

What the hell was Max's secret?

From: Max

I go on in five. I feel like I'm stepping out there
in my underwear. I'm nervous as shit!!
Wish you were here, Jap.

9:33 pm 4/22/06

chapter seven

Stand-up comedy is the closest thing to real justice you're going to find." Lucien Nutt was talking.

Max Biaggi Jr. was listening.

"You fuck around with the audience, you're going down. If you don't believe in your own stuff one hundred percent, you can't sell it."

Max nodded to the beat of the old pro's wisdom. "Well, Gramps, I wish we'd had this little talk a week ago, because I've got, like, one or two good bits, and the rest is shit."

Lucien chuckled. "Well, kid, get big enough laughs on those bits, and you just might make it off the stage alive." Impulsively, he pulled Max in for a bear hug.

The crusty old bastard reeked of cigar smoke and Jack Daniel's, but Max considered this spontaneous affection to be warm and comforting. It was everything he never got from his own parents.

Max had returned from New York with an exciting agenda and a more serious approach to his future. If there had been one lesson learned during spring break, it was that life could *not* be taken for granted.

Sho's overdose had taught him that. So had Vanity's ordeal with Jayson "J.J." James. And Christina's brush with death on the rooftop was something to reflect on, as well.

All the deep thinking led him to ask one question of paramount importance: What the hell was he doing with his life? Besides living for the next party and the next sex act, Max had no immediate answer.

Until one week ago. Max had been bored as hell on a Saturday night and decided to take in Bill Bellamy's late-night set at the Improv. Going alone allowed him the indulgence of soaking up the experience.

And he loved it—the belligerent crowd, the watered-down drinks, the bad food, the anxious please-God-don't-let-me-bomb comedians, the tense atmosphere, the stench of wood and cigarettes. It was awesome.

Not to mention serendipitous. The beer-sloshed flyer on Max's table had instantly arrested his attention. START YOUR COMEDY CAREER TODAY: PRIVATE STAND-UP CLASSES.

The idea conjured up secret yearnings from yesteryear. Max had long held a desire to be a comedian. And it was more than just his friends laughing at him all the time that triggered it. Down deep, the passion was there. But he knew the world of stand-up could be brutal. And for the rich son of a famous movie star, it would be even more brutal. No matter, the events of spring break were propelling him to move beyond his comfort zone.

Signing up for the classes had been the easy part. After all, Lucien Nutt was the teacher, and the man was a comic legend, having appeared not only as a regular guest with Jay Leno, David Letterman, and Conan O'Brien, but as a featured player in scores of television sitcoms and big-screen gross-out comedies, usually typecast in the role of the horny grandfather.

Lucien had worked one-on-one with Max, mentoring him on the finer points of tapping into his voice, finding his true persona, and developing a stylized, confident stage presence. The five-day stint was a crash course, to be sure. Still, Max could never remember feeling quite this excited about anything.

Maybe the reason was finding a creative outlet that he owned lock, stock, and punch line. Or maybe it was the simple adrenaline. Just walking out on that stage was telling every member of the audience, "Yeah, motherfucker, I'm funny. Get ready to laugh." That took a huge set of balls.

And he needed them right now. By the end of Max's first week of private instruction, Lucien had been so impressed with his progress that he convinced the Improv's manager to give him a five-minute newbie spotlight.

So here he was, in the same spot where Jerry Seinfeld, Ellen DeGeneres, Jim Carrey, and Dave Chappelle had once stood, waiting for his cue to take the mic on a Saturday night at the Improv. Crazy shit!

There were a few other wannabes hanging around. Out of their mouths came words of well wishes, but the message blazing from their eyes said something along the lines of, "I hope you crash and burn, asshole." Jealousy among comedians was insane.

One guy went by the name Spasm. His routine consisted mainly of Tourette's-like outbursts and weird body convulsions. It rarely garnered anything but a few modest giggles at the beginning. But Spasm refused to rethink his act. He was dark, moody, and impossible to interact with, yet still a club fixture at all hours.

Another regular was Vicky Crow, a morbidly obese woman pushing thirty who would do or say anything at her own expense for a laugh. Her bit about having time to eat a whole pie while a man struggled through layers of fat to find her vagina was an audience favorite. But Max thought she was a psycho and kept his distance. Especially after she went bug fuck on him for reaching out to take one of her cheese fries.

His favorite upstart was Tyrese Jones, a cool black guy with the razor-sharp mind of a Chris Rock and the cover boy looks of a young Denzel Washington. Women went ape shit for Tyrese. He was a notorious pussy hound, too. The revolving door of one-night stands and attendant girl dramas made for not only a great spectator sport, but also rich material for the dude's stage act.

Lucien's avuncular regard for Max had stirred up plenty of seething resentment. Everybody sought the old guy's approval, not only because of his influence at the club, but for the fact that getting a nod from a comic at his experience level was a major vote of confidence. His private classes were expensive, though. Spasm, Vicky, and Tyrese could barely afford to pay their rent, so the sour opinion floated that Max was buying his way onto the stage.

He checked himself before he started to whine about the perils of being rich. So what if a few dirt-poor twats were giving him shit? He would still rather be flush with megabucks. Rushing into one of those payday advance joints to keep a cellphone in service was no way to live. And that's exactly what Spasm had had to do just a few days ago.

"We're ready for you, Lucien."

Max tensed up and shot a look to the announcer, but the man was already gone.

Lucien squeezed Max's shoulder. "This is it, kid. If you need to puke, do it now. Comics who lose their last meal on the stage never get asked back."

Max managed a weak grin. "I'm good. But thanks."

"Remember what we talked about," Lucien advised. "Open, sustain, and pace yourself. Five minutes can be a goddamn eternity up there."

Max shook his head up and down, swallowing hard. Reluctantly, he stepped over to the curtain and surreptitiously peered out at the audience.

Christ. No headliner on the bill and the room was still packed. Word had traveled that Dane Cook might drop in over the weekend to test new material. For now, though, the suckers would have to settle for Max Biaggi Jr.

He swept the area for familiar faces. Suddenly, he smiled. Sitting dead center near the front of the stage were Shoshanna, Dante, Vanity, and Pippa. No matter how bad he sucked tonight, Max could at least count on big laughs from that table.

Just two weeks after her overdose, Shoshanna was back to the same precocious vamp style, causing a stir in her ass-cheek-baring Judy shorts by Seven Jeans and a weathered cotton tee that screamed BAD GIRLS SUCK, REAL GIRLS SWALLOW. But as far as Max was concerned, Sho would be on a short leash until her thirtieth birthday. So the upscale slut look was just that—a look.

Vanity and Dante held court as the hottest couple in the club. By comparison, Angelina Jolie and Brad Pitt were just two ordinary people. Dante kept a possessive hand on Vanity's Paige denim-clad thigh, occasionally whispering in her ear and stealing a kiss. He was gone. So was she. It was a total love wreck. Of course, Simon St. John hated their union. How did a father get over the fact that a boy he considered trash was nailing his daughter on a regular basis? Max wondered this with a wicked sense of glee. Why? Because if anyone deserved that special kind of torment, then it was Vanity's worthless dad.

Max noticed that Pippa had positioned her chair slightly away from the group. She just sat there with a vacant expression on her face, not interacting with the others unless spoken to. Of course, it was a miracle that she had even shown up at all. Max counted his blessings for that, though her behavior continued to mystify him.

Before spring break, she had been generally unavailable, but still the same saucy girl he had fallen three-quarters in love with. Now she was nothing more than an emotionally empty vessel growing increasingly distant from her friends.

But the real puzzle was the disappearance of Christina. Without explanation, she had just vanished. Cellphone calls, texts, and emails went unanswered. When Max called her mother, the political barracuda had been vague on the girl's whereabouts, only offering that she was visiting family out of state and would be unreachable for the next few weeks.

Shit! Had a time machine taken her back to the frontier era? Who could be "unreachable" in the year 2006? None of it made any sense. Her absence was a true disappointment, too. He really wanted Jap here to support him tonight.

"Do your thing, man. Just go out there and do your thing," Tyrese said.

Max gave him a cool nod. He sucked in a deep breath, then glanced around to see Spasm staring daggers at him and Vicky destroying a platter of chicken tenders, fish fingers, and mozzarella sticks.

Lucien was already on the stage, halfway into Max's introduction. "So I've been working with this young comic, and he's not the worst punk I've ever dealt with. I spent a few days giving him pointers and never once felt like carving him up with a meat cleaver."

A low rumble of laughter erupted from the crowd.

"And from an old-timer to a young buck, that's the closest thing to love you'll find in this business," Lucien went on. "Keep in mind—tonight is this guy's first time out. He's a stand-up virgin. So don't scare off the little prick. Put your hands together for *Max B*!"

There was a moment—coinciding with the welcoming

applause from the crowd—when Max thought about racing out of the building, jumping into his car, and never coming back. But instead he stepped into the spotlight, determined to see this through, not only to make Lucien proud, but to prove something to himself, too.

If nothing else, he knew that he looked good in his AG jeans and Morphine Generation hoodie. The look was hot without trying too hard. The idea to drop the radioactive last name for the simple initial B had been his. Winning over a crowd was hard enough without frontloading a performance with the surname Biaggi and all the preconceived notions that came along with it.

He approached the mic, greeted the audience, and launched into his first routine about drunken late-night food binges. It was bombing. But Max kept his cool. Stage survival rule number one: When a joke doesn't work, never take it out on the crowd.

"Okay, that sucked. I'm a big freaking *loser!*"

He got some mild laughs this time. Self-abuse always pulled them to your side.

"You know, I haven't gotten laid in a few months. I used to get sex all the time. My parents never trusted me to be at home alone with a girl, but once my grandmother moved in with us, everything was cool, because she would chaperone. There was one hard-and-fast rule—no private time in my bedroom with a girl. We had to stay in the living room with Grandma. This worked out real good on account of the fact that this woman was so out of it. I mean, she never knew what the hell was going on! I got my first blow job and lost my virginity with Grandma in the same room. And all she ever told my parents was, 'Max is a good boy.' " He delivered the last line in the voice of an old woman. "Damn right I was good! Kim Foster came home from school with me every day for a month!"

Serious chuckles erupted.

Max felt the energy. They liked him. They liked Max B. They liked this bit. He pressed on, feeling the uptick of excitement. "Well, Grandma died . . ."

The audience responded with an exaggerated, mournful moan.

Max couldn't help but smile. They were into it. Man, this felt good. Now he nodded somberly. "Yeah, it was a sad day . . . especially when I realized later on that I couldn't get it up without an old lady in the room. Take it from me, when you're coming on to a girl, that can be a tough sell."

The room exploded with laughter. Loud, raucous bursts. Hands slapping the tables. The whole shebang. Max B, a terrified first-timer, had killed them on a Saturday night at the Improv.

"Thank you, everybody." He raised a hand.

The crowd gave him a quick round of hearty applause.

As he exited the stage, he made eye contact with a pretty blonde, who gave him the kind of look that promoted hope for the night ahead. He grinned. The funny guy never went home alone.

Lucien was right there, ready with a hug and a slap on the back. "It started out rocky, but you recovered. I'm proud of you, kid. You've got some chops. You still need a lot of work. But you've got some natural chops."

Max beamed, feeling ten feet tall.

Tyrese stepped over and pulled Max in for a fast embrace. "You're a slayer, man."

Max let out a huge breath as if to expel all of his anxiety. "Shit, I don't know. For a minute there at the beginning . . ."

Vicky spoke up. "Wasn't that a new bit?" It was more of an accusation than a question.

"Yeah," Max said, wondering where she was going with this.

"Everybody knows it's a mistake to open with new material," Vicky sneered. "That's *basic*."

"General nutrition is basic, too," Max countered. "So why the hell do you think deep-fried batter is a major food group?"

Tyrese doubled over in laughter.

Twin patches of red splotched Vicky's fat cheeks.

Max knew it was a cheap shot, but it was important to

establish a reputation for being brutal in even casual battle. Otherwise, comics would eat you alive and mess with your head whenever they got the chance.

Across the room, Spasm glared at Max with an unsettling, quietly intense fury. Crazy bastard. Max ignored him and made a move into the main room, anxious to see his real friends.

Dante stood up and pumped Max's hand with a firm shake that came close to disconnecting his shoulder. "That was awesome, dude! Somebody bring this bitch a beer!"

A perky waitress was already there with a Michelob Lite. "Great set, Max."

"Thanks, Gigi."

Her stare lingered for a moment too long. Finally, she moved on, and Dante watched her disappear. "She seems especially attentive. Did you nail her?"

Max shot a backward glance to Gigi, who had stopped to glare at them. Now he felt like an asshole, and for once he wasn't guilty of the charge. "Keep your voice down, man. She's a good girl."

Dante's eyebrows shot up.

"How good?"

Vanity reached for the growth on Dante's goatee and yanked hard.

"Ouch!" Then Dante gave her a smoldering look. "Hurt me, baby, hurt me."

Vanity rolled her eyes. "Max is growing up, and you're regressing. I didn't sign up for this crap."

Everybody laughed.

Max turned to Pippa. "What's up, mystery girl? Thanks for coming. I'm glad you made it."

She managed a weak smile. "Wouldn't miss it for the world. You were nang."

In response, Max puffed out his chest and assumed a cocky stance. "Did you hear that, Sho? I'm 'nang.' "

His sister jumped up to wrap her arms around him and kiss his cheek. "Congratulations. I thought you'd completely suck, but you were actually kind of funny." One beat. "Now can I please have a real drink? I'm sick of Diet Coke."

Max turned up his beer and guzzled almost half of it. "You're underage."

Shoshanna fumed defiantly. "So are you!"

Max shrugged. "Well, try to go one month without slipping into a coma. Then we'll see about you."

Shoshanna made a minidrama out of fishing for her cellular. "I'm calling Yummy. She'll come get me and take me somewhere that's not so lame."

Max shook his head. "Easy, party girl. The only place you're going is home to bed. *Alone.*"

Dante hooked an arm around Vanity and pulled her close. "We'll take her. We're getting ready to bolt anyway. You deserve to hang out and celebrate."

Vanity nodded her agreement.

Max regarded them with a mixture of gratitude and annoyance. Dante and Vanity were at that self-absorbed stage in a couple's first blush of togetherness, when they only needed and wanted to be around each other.

"God, this sucks!" Shoshanna grumbled.

"Come on," Dante said easily. "It's not so bad. We'll stop for ice cream."

Shoshanna rolled her eyes to heaven. "Ooh, and maybe after that you can take me for a pony ride."

Vanity collected her metallic pewter Chloe bag and moved in to kiss Max lightly on the lips, smelling sweetly of Jo Malone's Nectarine Blossom and Honey cologne. "You did great up there tonight. But I want to talk to you about something. It's important. Call me tomorrow, okay?"

Max nodded, intrigued. As Dante, Vanity, and Shoshanna filed out, he slipped into a chair next to Pippa.

She feigned a yawn. "I should probably go, too."

Max glanced down at his Rolex. "Why? It's still early."

"I'm tired," Pippa said. "Besides, I'm sure you have loads of chirping to do. I'll just be in the way."

Max looked at her. In Pippa Keith parlance, "chirping" meant chatting up girls. "I'd rather spend some time with you."

She stood up to leave. "I think you'd have much more fun with Gigi the waitress."

"We used to have fun."

As Pippa fell silent, a certain sadness skated across her face. "We did, didn't we?"

Max grinned. "You used to call begging me to take you out, because you were *bored rigid*." He did his best Pippa impression on the last bit.

She smiled. "I don't think I ever quite begged exactly."

"Oh, it was begging," Max insisted lightly.

Pippa refused to give in. "Maybe a pretty please."

Max reached out for her hand. "Come on. How long has it been since—"

Pippa pulled fast and firm from his grasp. Instantly, she appeared to regret the hostile move. "Sorry . . . I—"

But Max was already offended. "Don't worry about it."

He started to take off.

"Max, wait!" Pippa pleaded.

He halted and spun around to face her. "For what?"

"I didn't mean to—"

"Forget it." His tone was like acid.

"But I don't want—"

"You don't want *me*, Pippa," Max cut in. "I get that loud and clear. When you needed someone to pick up all the tabs, and you needed to get from point A to point B in a Porsche, I was good enough company. But you've got your own ride now." He swept a hand up and down to point out her expensive Roberto Cavalli halter dress. "And you obviously don't have money troubles. Although sometimes I wonder how you earn it."

Pippa glared at him. "Oh, we're back to that again, are we?" She grabbed her Alexander McQueen satchel, holding it up as faux evidence. "Pippa has a nice handbag, so she must be a hooker."

"Who is this 'entertainment promoter' that you work for?" Max challenged.

"That's confidential." Pippa sniffed.

Max lifted his brow and snarled. "Yeah, usually those kind of arrangements are."

Pippa's eyes blazed with fury, and when she spoke, it was in a cold, almost sinister voice. "Trust me, Max. You *don't* want to know where my money comes from. I'm protecting you, because you couldn't handle it. You're much better off in the dark with your point money and your rich-kid toys and your third-rate comedy act."

"I didn't realize whores could be such harsh critics," Max shot back. "I considered my act at least second rate."

"Go to hell," Pippa said. And then she stalked out of the Improv.

He watched her leave, knowing that what had been on life support was now officially dead. They were over. Done. Finished for good. But the last thing Max intended to do was sulk about it like a little bitch.

Sweeping a gaze around the club, he noticed the same

pretty blonde from before. A few more beers, a willing girl . . . not the worst way to end a night.

Max boldly slipped past the gay best friend to make his approach. "Do we know each other?"

The grin on her face was playful. "I don't know, do we?"

Max always enjoyed the game. "I would remember if I saw you naked."

She laughed at him. "Has that line ever worked?"

"Is it working now?"

She shook her head. "Not really."

"Okay, how about this one: I'm good-looking, funny, my Porsche is parked out front, and you can order anything you want from room service."

The blonde's eyes sparkled.

"How's that line working?"

"Much better."

"I'm Max."

"I'm Strawberry."

He nodded, loving her name. "*Sweet.*"

She gave him a sexy look. "You have no idea."

Max excused himself to say his good-byes to Lucien, then returned to claim his fruit of the night. Together they tumbled into his ride and zipped out of the Shoppes of Mayfair parking lot on a highly charged erotic mission.

Sanctuary was one of Miami's newest boutique hotels,

an exclusive thirty-room oasis that provided necessary relief from the wild decadence of South Beach.

He drove like a speed demon, rocking "Dani California" by the Red Hot Chili Peppers at maximum decibels, the altercation with Pippa a distant memory.

The hotel was tucked away on James Avenue, a quiet residential side street between Seventeenth and Eighteenth, just off Collins Avenue and a mere block from the ocean and the city's rabid club scene.

Max surrendered the Porsche to the valet and rushed Strawberry up to his "ultra-luxury" suite. Clothing disappeared. And that's when the real fun began. A steamy collision of hungry, pleasure-seeking bodies.

Max lost himself in Strawberry's juicy sweetness. When it was over, he rolled onto his stomach and sighed out his satisfaction. "That was awesome." For a moment, he basked in the afterglow, the intense orgasm still tingling his nerve endings.

"I want pancakes," Strawberry announced. "Do you think room service has pancakes?"

The sexual thrill evaporated. Just like that. Max's mind took him right back to the Improv, right back to his fight with Pippa. God, he missed that girl like crazy. And all the Strawberries in the world would never help him forget her.

He got up and slipped on the complimentary robe

hanging in the bathroom. "Order anything you want. I'll be back in a few."

"Where are you going?" Strawberry whined.

Max didn't answer. He just took in a breath, exhaling slowly as he closed the door and made his way to the rooftop pool, suddenly desperate to be alone. The meltdown with Pippa had his mind in overdrive.

You don't want to know where my money comes from. I'm protecting you, because you couldn't handle it.

Max wondered what the hell she had meant by that. And he would never stop wondering until he found out.

A male couple frolicked in the pool—a paunchy, older executive type and his chiseled boy toy.

Max did a double take, suddenly recognizing the younger guy.

It was Carb Duffy, Christina's Chippendales friend from New York.

"More champagne!" the old man sang, giggling indulgently as he exited the pool and waddled toward one of the oversize teak cabanas, leaving Carb alone to wade in the water.

Max approached the pool's edge.

Carb glanced up. His face registered real surprise. "Small world."

Max gave him a smug look. "Yeah, too small."

There was a long stretch of silence as Carb thought of

something else to say. "How's Christina? I programmed my number into her cell, but she never called. Maybe she hasn't noticed it yet."

Max shrugged. "She's off on some mysterious family retreat."

"So her mother did make her go," Carb remarked knowingly. "That's sad. I think those programs are sick."

Max narrowed his eyes. "What are you talking about?"

"She told me her mother was making her go to some center in Mississippi that promises to de-gay teenagers."

Max shook his head, refusing to believe it. "You've got to be bullshitting me."

But Carb's expression was sincere. "No, that's exactly what she said."

"Jesus Christ," Max muttered. Suddenly, he felt a seething resentment toward Carb. Yes, this was the guy who had saved Jap, but he was also the guy she had chosen to confide in. "Why would she tell you this instead of me?"

Carb shrugged. "I don't know. I wouldn't read too much into it, though. Sometimes people find it easier to confess things to total strangers."

"Oh, a psychiatrist *and* a rent boy," Max snapped. "I didn't realize you were such a multitalent." He stormed back to the suite, dressed quickly, and left Strawberry alone to wait for her stupid pancakes.

Max drove like a maniac all the way to Star Island, his mind locked on a single track. Where had Paulina Perez sent Christina?

He would *definitely* find out.

From: Max

Jap, if you get this, PLEASE text back. Paulina,
if you happen to be reading, let me go on record
as saying that you're a smelly cunt with the
maternal instincts of a piranha.

11:19 pm 4/22/06

chapter eight

Mississippi was beautiful, tranquil . . . and suffocating to the point of being almost deadly.

The view from Christina's window revealed a sea of tall pines. She sat on the twin bed inside her small private room at Salvation Pointe and gazed out, marveling at nature's handiwork, imagining ways to kill herself.

But Christina planned to wait until she returned home, because the end game was to have Paulina find her body and live miserably with the horror and guilt. Being told that her daughter had committed suicide at Salvation Pointe would be too easy on her bitch of a mother.

Thoughts about how to do it consumed her. She wanted the discovery to be particular grisly. The importance of creating an indelible image of death was key. Perhaps that's why the option of slitting her wrists seemed to be the enduring method of choice. The blood flow alone would make the scene unforgettable.

Three fast knocks rapped the open door.

Christina turned around to see Zack Webber.

"Time for afternoon therapy," he sang. "Wait. That sounded gay." He tried to imitate the voice of Darth Vader. "*Time for afternoon therapy.*" One beat. "Is that butch enough?"

Christina laughed.

Zack was her favorite resident/patient/inmate at Salvation Pointe. He had been dispatched here from Granite, Utah, by order of his father, a syndicated talk radio personality.

Zack wanted to be a ballet dancer, he loved *Gilmore Girls*, and he lacked any interest or acumen in team sports. For the fifteen-year-old son of a conservative who hosted a show called *Man to Man with Dick Webber*, those telltale signs of potential homosexuality were apparently grounds for aggressive intervention. So here Zack was.

He stepped over to Christina's desk and inspected a beaded bracelet she had made in one of her craft classes. "This is cute."

"Boys shouldn't wear jewelry," Christina scolded him jokingly.

"*Sorry*, I forgot," Zack replied with snide alarm, dropping the delicate piece immediately. "A bracelet could mean that I'm gay." He sighed. "Do you want to know the most ironic thing? My macho dad sent me to this awful place, and he hosts a show called *Man to Man with Dick Webber*, which is the *gayest* sounding title I've ever heard!"

Christina cackled.

Zack rolled his eyes. "Oh, well. We've only got one more week, right?"

She gave him an upbeat nod, even though the time left loomed like an eternal torture sentence.

"It seems like we were just in group," Zack grumbled.

"That's because we were," Christina said. "And there's still evening group after this."

He groaned. "Did I tell you that I got assigned to private counseling, too?"

Christina shook her head.

"Apparently, the 'pace of my progress' is troubling, so Chet Hobbs is working with me one-on-one."

"In addition to group?"

Zack nodded.

The news made Christina wonder if she might be targeted for private sessions, as well. Of course, the more important question was this: When would they fit it in?

The Salvation Pointe staff operated the facility's schedule with military precision. There was a six o'clock wake-up call, breakfast, fifteen minutes to shower, morning group therapy, Bible study, a walk around the lake, lunch, cards and board games, private reflection time, afternoon group therapy, more Bible study, crafts for girls and football for boys, dinner, a bike ride, evening group therapy, another Bible study, and, finally, lights out at nine o'clock sharp. Day in, day out. No changes whatsoever.

Zack let out a bored sigh. "If we don't hurry, we're going to be late, and you know what that means—cleanup detail after dinner."

But Christina lingered, her body practically refusing to move. She regarded her funny young friend with his tall frame, gangly limbs, and delicate facial features that crossed the border of handsome and ventured into the land of pretty. "Zack, is any of this working for you?"

He considered the question. "Is that a polite way of asking me if I suddenly want to play wide receiver and make out with a cheerleader?"

Christina grinned at him.

"To tell you the truth, I don't know why I'm here. People have been calling me a sissy or a faggot since kindergarten, but I've never so much as kissed a boy. They want to *un*gay me, but I'm not even sure if I *am* gay. I think guys are cute. I think girls are cute. But I've never really felt overtly sexual urges for anybody. I guess that makes me a freak."

"Don't think that way," Christina told him. "You're not a freak."

Zack's face darkened with sadness. "Tell that to my dad." He slumped down into the cheap desk chair. "I just want to be left alone, you know? All I want to do is dance and watch *Gilmore Girls*. Who does that hurt exactly?"

"Nobody," Christina answered quietly.

Zack shook his head wearily. "I've been fighting the same fight since I was five, and each year it only seems to get worse. The week before I came here some guys at school took all the foil from their hot dogs, molded it into the shape of a penis, and shoved it in my mouth in front of the entire cafeteria."

Christina's heart suddenly felt heavy. "Oh, Zack," she whispered, reaching out to touch his arm as tears formed in his eyes.

"That was the tipping point for my dad. Later that night I heard him telling my mom that he didn't want a queer son. He said that I was going to Salvation Pointe and that he'd send me back here as many times as it took to make the program stick."

Christina gave him a quizzical look.

"Most kids go through the program at least three times," Zack explained. "I don't want to come back, but I'm sure I'll get stuck here again during the summer."

Christina was absolutely stunned.

"It's true. I mean, take Jordan. I know for a fact that this is his *fifth* residency."

Christina had no idea. And she routinely walked around the lake in a small group that included him. Jordan Thiessen was a sweet, overweight, sixteen-year-old from Georgia who loved musicals. "That's insane."

Zack shrugged helplessly. "The salespeople do a great job of preparing parents for that. Personally, I think it's a revenue scam."

"It *is* a scam!" Christina raged. "And the therapies are bogus. Is anybody here licensed? I haven't seen any credentials. We spend hours in so-called 'treatment,' but none of the counselors have any formal education or training! I don't care if Chet Hobbs presides over the largest church in the state. Does he have the clinical background to deal with adolescents on complicated issues of sexuality?"

Zack responded with a defeated shrug. "He's clergy, and the program is Christian-based. Everything they do here is protected under the First Amendment."

Christina balled up her fists and hammered them down on the mattress. "This has to be exposed! There should be state regulations! There should be federal sanctions!"

But Zack appeared neither moved nor motivated by her fury. "Who's going to fight for a bunch of gay teenagers?"

It was phrased as a rhetorical question. But Christina instantly knew the answer. Keiko would fight for them. QUAN! would fight for them. Queers Unite for Action Now! was precisely the sort of extreme advocacy group to infiltrate and wage war on Salvation Pointe. If Keiko knew about this place, then she would be foaming at the mouth to cause trouble. Anything rooted in the establishment stirred the Japanese girl's most militant impulses.

Forgiving Keiko for all of the deceptions came easily; Christina had already made peace with that. And now, in a strange way, she understood the activist's take-no-prisoners mentality of conviction more clearly than ever.

Pretending to be seventeen when in fact she was twenty-seven. Befriending a Senate hopeful's closeted lesbian daughter. Using the personal as political in a media fight to expose hypocrisy. Shaming Paulina Perez's campaign to shut down school-sponsored gay/straight alliance clubs.

Yes, Christina had been a pawn in all of it, but the cause had been for the greater good. In Keiko's eyes, she had used and exploited one young person on a quest to improve the lives of maybe thousands more. And the truth was, Christina stood ready to be used again.

If it served to expose the reality about Salvation Pointe and to help innocent souls like Zack and Jordan, then so be it. Besides, her mother would get dragged through the muck of embarrassing headlines. And the cold bitch deserved to be forced off-message again.

Finally, Christina spoke. "I know who will fight for us." She felt her heartbeat pick up speed. "I just need to get to a phone or to a computer with Internet access."

"Easier said than done," Zack pointed out. "This place is like a prison."

Christina's mind raced, searching for an answer. At first, it seemed hopeless. After all, criminals doing hard time had more freedoms. Salvation Pointe forbade its residents everything from the outside world.

No closed doors (with the exception of fifteen minutes each day for showering).

No contact with friends or family.

No external news sources.

No music (unless preapproved Christian CDs or preloaded MP3-players provided by Salvation Pointe staff).

No television.

No Internet use.

No cellular phones.

No diary or journal writing.

Oh God! The straitjacket atmosphere infuriated Christina all over again as she mentally checked off the demoralizing prohibitions.

They wouldn't even let her draw. Not having that outlet had been excruciating. Sometimes just making rough sketches of a *Harmony Girl* story could transport Christina to a wonderful place. But Salvation Pointe considered such pursuits "subversive."

Every aspect of residents' lives here was so tightly bound. Still, somewhere there had to be an opening.

Suddenly, Zack's eyes brightened. "Maybe there's a way."

"What?" Christina demanded.

"My first private session with Chet Hobbs happened after bed check. We talked in a parlor room connected to his office, so his desk was unattended. He's got a Mac. He's got a phone." Zack raised his brow.

Christina considered the situation. "I just have to get past the night monitors."

"That's easy," Zack said. "Talk Richie into faking a panic attack. He'll do it. He's a drama queen. Just tell him it's the role of a lifetime. It'll make him feel like Scarlett Johansson."

Christina giggled. "When do you see Hobbs again?"

"Tomorrow night."

She nodded thoughtfully. Staring out at the impossibly green pines once more, she silently cursed herself for keeping this banishment to Salvation Pointe a secret. Paulina had laid out a perfect game plan of shame and manipulation, and Christina had played it exactly as her mother had intended.

Now she was trapped in this horrible place and no-body knew where she was. Never before had she felt so isolated, so marginalized, so helpless.

"Do you think this plan will work?"

Christina fixed a serious gaze on her new friend. "It has to, Zack. The people here are doing all of us more harm than good."

From: Mimi

PEOPLE is still interested in the exclusive, but they
need an answer. Otherwise we lose the cover.

9:02 am 4/23/06

chapter nine

but I like *your* sheets," Dante mumbled, smoothing a hand down the four hundred-thread count Egyptian cotton. He lay there nude, on his stomach, the top sheet barely covering his muscular ass.

For a moment, the sight took Vanity's breath away. He was a vision, every art director's wet dream with his café au lait skin against the brilliant superwhite of the bedding.

She crawled back in to lightly rake the inside of his forearm with her nails.

Dante responded with the slightest body tremor, murmuring, "Mmmm . . . that gives me chills."

"It's getting late," Vanity whispered. "You have to get up. You have to get dressed. You have to *go*."

Dante remained half-asleep. "Where am I supposed to go?"

"*Home.*" Lazily, she traced the outline of his tattoo with her fingertip.

"I don't have one." He rolled over, moving onto his back for a good stretch, a sexy grin planted on his face. "I'm homeless."

"Liar."

"It's true." He stroked her bare thigh. "I'm in need. Help me out."

He was so fucking hot. Vanity could see the sheet moving in her peripheral vision as it began to tent impressively with Dante's morning glory. God, she wanted to go after him like he was one big stick of candy. But right now there was no time.

"Come on," she said, slipping off the bed. "I'll give you a ride to the nearest shelter."

"Baby, please." He reached out, just missing her. "Where do you have to be on a Sunday?"

Vanity started to get dressed. "I told you. Dr. Parker's going away for two weeks, but she made time to see me this morning." She glanced at the clock. "At ten. Which is about the same time that my father's flight gets in from Los Angeles." She stepped into a pair of Etro satin pants and pulled a D&G chiffon blouse over her head. "I think those are two good reasons why you should go."

Dante cut a sly glance to the tepee at his crotch, then back to Vanity. "Do you have to leave right away?"

She just smiled at him, shaking her head. "We did it four times last night. I think you've got a problem."

"Yeah, well, last night you couldn't get enough of my problem."

"And I'm sure I'll want to be burdened with it again very soon. But right now I have to go." She blew him a kiss. "Lala made a huge breakfast. Eat fast. You know who is approaching Miami."

"That's all I get?" Dante complained. "Come over here and give me a real kiss good-bye. I'm working on a new track today. I need some inspiration."

Vanity tossed him a shrewd look. She was tempted. Very tempted. But it would only mean her clothes coming off and being late for her appointment. "Nice try. You almost had me." And then she dashed out, smiling so much that it almost made her face hurt.

She was still in the garage and fastening her seat belt when Mimi Blair called. Vanity picked up to say, "It's Sunday morning. Don't publicists go to church?"

"No," Mimi snapped. "And we don't sleep, either. All of us are agnostic insomniacs."

Vanity laughed.

"Listen, we need to discuss the *People* issue."

"I haven't made a decision yet."

"Not deciding is saying no," Mimi said impatiently. "If we don't commit now, we're going to lose the cover."

"Then I guess we've lost it."

Mimi was silent.

Vanity fired up her new black Spyker C8 Laviolette and zoomed off, feeling the awesome power of the Audi V8 engine.

"A *People* cover is a huge opportunity," Mimi finally said.

"Mimi, I know how this will play out, no matter what ground rules are set up in advance or how sensitive the writer pretends to be. I can already see the page layout in my head—a photo of my demolished Mercedes from the accident, screen captures from the sex tape, J.J.'s mug shot, and for good measure, they'll probably use one of my mother's old supermodel poses." She sighed. "I'm not interested in being merchandised that way."

"*Merchandised*?" Mimi was apoplectic. "Honey, we're talking about your life."

"Exactly. And I don't want it splashed across the pages of *People*."

"Vanity, this is the game," Mimi said evenly. "It's why you're a star. The public is fascinated. And believe me, they're not interested in every teen mess. Katee K's already stabbed her mother, but she'd have to stab the president of the United States to get half the attention that you earn. Fans are out there rooting for you."

"Do you really believe that?" Vanity asked. Her tone

carried the implicit message that "yes" would be the stupid answer.

"I do," Mimi said. "Stardom is a reciprocal enterprise. You give talent. You get fame. This is—"

Vanity cut her off. "What's *my* big talent?"

"Living a life that people want to know about." Mimi laughed a little. "Being beautiful and rich doesn't hurt, either. I guess that makes you a triple threat."

Vanity white-knuckled the steering wheel. She was *not* amused. "So people want to read about the gorgeous beach girl with money to burn. And they want all the dirt whenever I crash a car, drink too much, make a sex tape, or get kidnapped by a crackhead ex-boyfriend. Don't pee on my leg and call it rain, Mimi. You know the *real* game. It's not my life that interests people. It's my failures—the more embarrassing, the better. Fans aren't rooting for me as much as they're resenting me. And just for having looks and money, the very things they want for themselves. I don't want to feed into the media machine anymore. That's not who I am. That's not who I want to be."

"It doesn't have to be all or nothing," Mimi argued gently. "You can feed the media beast without sacrificing yourself to it. Haters are out there, that's true. But so are many young girls who admire you."

Vanity noticed her speed and eased it down.

"Let's brainstorm a new strategy."

Vanity sighed. Part of her wanted to fire Mimi Blair and just walk away. But another part wondered if this could be the beginning of a positive image reinvention.

Beep.

Max was calling.

"I'll think about it," Vanity promised. She signed off with Mimi and clicked over to Miami's newest Last Comic Standing. "I didn't expect to hear from you until at least two o'clock."

"I think Christina might be in trouble," Max said. His tone was dead serious.

Vanity's stomach dropped. "What kind of trouble?"

"She told the guy who saved her on the roof that her mother was sending her to one of those programs that promises to reverse gayness."

Vanity's mouth dropped open. "And you think she's there now?"

"That's what I'm afraid of. Paulina was evasive. She just told me Christina was visiting family and unreachable."

Vanity experienced a crashing sense of guilt. She knew Christina had been deeply troubled by something last week, but hadn't pressed hard enough to find out what.

"Max, I don't like the sound of this. I've heard scary things about those programs."

"Same here. This guy swears that she told him the

place was in Mississippi, but I spent half the night on Google and couldn't find anything."

Vanity weaved in and out of slower-moving traffic, maintaining speed, thinking fast. All of a sudden, the solution came to mind. "Keiko."

"What about her?" Max asked, his tone hostile. "If it wasn't for that—"

Vanity stopped him. "Keiko could find her, Max. Think about it. The mission of QUAN! is to fight against programs like this. And I'm sure they have resources and networks that go far beyond a laptop and a Google search."

Max fell silent.

"I know how much you hate her . . ." Vanity said.

"Yeah . . . but maybe that sushi bitch can redeem herself. I think the main office is in San Francisco. I'll try there first."

Vanity was taken aback by his ferocious concern. She had never thought of Max as a caretaker before. But he seemed to be morphing into the role of everyone's protective older brother.

This realization was at once heartwarming and bittersweet. Nothing was the same anymore. Nothing would ever be the same again. Everybody was changing so much.

"Six kegs and no cops! Now that's a rager!" The Phi Delta Theta had a Coors in one hand, a vodka shot in the other, and both eyes on Pippa as he shouted to his brothers. "This girl's no skank, dude! She's freaking hot!"

Pippa knew the drill. Sunday after the Saturday-night frat party. Drunken idiots not ready to wind down. But it was no problem. She could handle losers who took their Cheerios with beer instead of milk in her sleep.

"Keep your drink just give me the money/It's just you and your hand tonight."

The hard-driving Pink track from *I'm Not Dead* rocked.

Pippa grooved to the cynicism of the lyrics and flipped upside down on the pole, spreading her legs wide, a true acrobatic move.

The worthless dirtbags went crazy.

"Hey, baby, I think I'm in love!" The same one was yelling. "Do you clean house, too?"

His buddies howled.

Like that was some original shit. Pippa had heard it a million times before. But a pack of dumb guys would laugh at anything.

She was just going through the motions now, marking time, trying to make as much money as possible before graduation. Because on that day, Star Baby was leaving Miami. And she was *never* coming back.

The cool million was hers, but that was security for the future. Pippa still needed cash for the present. So no matter how miserable the job, it made sense to continue dancing.

There were reasons of far greater importance, too. Keeping Vinnie happy, for one. Learning that his precious Star Baby was leaving Cheetah would rattle his cage something good. It would be foolish to quit until she stood ready to flee Miami immediately. Another work benefit was the simple distraction. It kept Pippa's mind occupied on subjects other than the mess of things she had made with Max.

Word of her violent encounter with Hellcat in the parking lot had spread throughout Cheetah. Now the other strippers regarded Pippa as something of a crazy, unpredictable badass and chose to keep their distance.

Pippa hardly went home and cried about it. The truth was, being odd girl out suited her just fine. She was looking out for number one, and relationships only got in the way.

The club was slipping. As a rule, Scores on Biscayne Boulevard had hotter girls and better dancers, not to mention a national reputation for quality and a more upscale atmosphere.

So Vinnie, money-grubbing son of a bitch that he was, decided to pump up the Cheetah revenue streams in illegal ways. The Lair had become a prostitution den where sexual acts were crudely negotiated for cash. In fact, Max

Biaggi was up there right now with Peppermint, Vinnie's new favorite, a Honduran girl with a barbell clitoral piercing.

Even drugs—once considered grounds for immediate termination—had entered the sleaze equation with Cheetah's own bartender pulling double duty as a go-to guy for OxyContin. Several girls called it "hillbilly heroin" and had taken to snorting it before going onstage.

Pippa didn't care. So what if the club environment was on a fast slide down? Star Baby was on short time with a million-dollar trust fund. And when she walked out, she would be moving on to a better tomorrow.

Consulting a financial attorney of her own had been a smart maneuver. Max Biaggi and his four-hundred-dollar-an-hour legal eagle got banged up good by Elaine Goldberg. She was a female, Jewish attorney: tough and mother-tiger protective.

By deal's end, Pippa had an ironclad irrevocable trust with a spendthrift clause. This limited the payout to small amounts at specified intervals until Pippa turned forty, at which point she assumed control of the fund.

"This is your future, gorgeous," Elaine had advised her. "No girl your age needs access to a million dollars. You'll either squander it by the time you're twenty-five, or you'll hand it off to the first asshole you fall in love with when he tells you about his great investment idea. And by the way, those always turn to shit. I've seen it happen too many times. Trust me. This is the best way."

And deep down, Pippa knew that it was. She never wanted to end up like her poor mum, Sophie Keith— divorced, broke, renting a dodgy cottage, always working and for crap pay at a start-up cable network. INT was gasping for ratings, so when she wasn't taping *The Frugal Designer: South Beach Style*, Sophie practically lived on the road, doing coast-to-coast shopping mall demonstrations to drum up viewer interest.

Pippa vowed never to be a victim like that. She loved her mum dearly, but at the same time, she resented her for not protecting herself and her daughter. Financial desperation only led to bad choices. Hello! A little foresight and fortitude please, especially with a child in tow.

The ugliness of it all made Pippa feel much older than her seventeen years. When she gazed in the mirror, sometimes she wondered who was looking back. The cold, hardened, humorless girl had to be a stranger.

I didn't realize whores could be such harsh critics.

Max's voice rang inside her head as the what-ifs churned inside her. What if Pippa had ignored the poor-girl pride to make her own money? What if she had given it a go with the rich-boy flirt? Would they still be together?

Pippa shook off the thought. Bygones. It didn't matter anymore. She'd set out to reclaim all the things that had been ripped away from her back in England—designer clothes, expensive handbags, dazzling jewelry, exquisite shoes. Everything she wanted was hers again. Including a personal asset report with six zeros on it. So why was she more miserable than ever?

"Do you have change for a five, baby?" It was the rowdy frat bastard again. "I'm going to need four-fifty back."

His brethren whooped and hollered.

Pippa regarded all of them like the seven damn good reasons for abortion that they were.

"This is a raid!" The shout came from a patron near the bar. He was suddenly flashing a badge.

What happened next shocked her into total paralysis. Pippa stood there, frozen onstage, gripping the cold steel of the metal pole with both hands, unable to let go as the events seemed to unfold in slow motion.

The OxyContin-dealing bartender got slammed face-down onto the counter and promptly handcuffed.

Uniformed police stormed the premises.

Total chaos ensued.

"If I'm going to jail, I better see what you've got first!" It was the frat boy leader. He bounded onto the stage and ripped the G-string from Pippa's body, leaving her naked from the waist down.

She screamed bloody murder.

He twirled the thong around an index finger, proudly showing it off to his buddies sitting front and center.

Pippa jammed her knee into his crotch, kicked hard, and gave the stunned college pig a powerful shove.

He went tumbling off the stage and onto the floor, landing awkwardly on one hand. The sickening crack had to be his wrist breaking. "Aaawwww!" The agonized wail confirmed it.

Two more plainclothes officers revealed themselves and marched up to the Lair. Within moments, Max Biaggi and Peppermint were being led downstairs, their hands shackled.

"You!"

Pippa spun around to see a policeman lurching toward her, a pair of cuffs at the ready. In a moment of sheer panic, she tried to flee.

But he moved too fast. "You're under arrest for public exposure of a sexual organ."

"No, you don't understand! I was attacked!" Pippa cried. There was a loud *clink* as the metal closures locked into place, painfully pinching her wrists.

"You have the right to remain silent . . ."

From: Dante

Love u. Miss u. Can't wait 2 kiss u.

10:47 am 4/23/06

chapter ten

I t's different," Vanity said. "When I've been in relationships before . . . I've never felt this way about myself."

"How is that?" Dr. Parker asked.

"I feel like I'm *okay*, you know? I feel open to be who I really am."

"So you feel accepted where you are?"

Vanity considered this. "It's more than that." She sighed. God, it was so frustrating when you couldn't articulate your feelings in therapy. Of all places to lose command of the English language. Finally, she found some verbal traction. "Dante has seen me at my worst. He's been face-to-face with my monster. And he still loves me." Her voice broke on the last bit. "It's strange . . . to feel safe enough to relax, to not worry about the threat of discovery . . . I've never experienced that before." She wiped away a tear with her fingers.

Dr. Parker leaned in to offer a tissue. "Explain what you mean by 'the threat of discovery.' "

Vanity took a deep breath and blotted her eyes. "I've always felt like there was a part of myself that I had to keep hidden—from boyfriends, from friends, from family. Dante has seen that part of me." She shook her head ruefully. "More than once. But he still wants me. He still wants us. I mean, let's face it, I bring a lot of baggage to a relationship."

"Everybody shows up with baggage," Dr. Parker pointed out. "Dante included."

"I know. But I've practically got my own fucking conveyor belt."

Dr. Parker laughed. "I've never heard it quite put that way before."

Vanity shrugged. "It's not just my excess baggage, either. There's my father and this controversy about an artist on his label stealing one of Dante's song ideas. It's a huge hit, too, so the issue never really goes away. Dante got screwed royally, but he let it go. For the sake of us."

Dr. Parker stared back thoughtfully, saying nothing.

Vanity continued to talk. "It's one thing to get involved with someone and then be confronted with demons later on. There's that moment when you have to decide, do I stay, or do I cut and run? But Dante committed to me after the fact. He had all the evidence in front of him. There wasn't a magic honeymoon to reflect back on. And he still chose me."

Dr. Parker smiled. "You have a lot to offer. He sounds like a smart guy."

Vanity could feel her heart swell as she thought more about it. "This feels like my first relationship. I don't know. It's just . . . *real*. God, it's almost boring. That's how real it is." She laughed a little. "Last night we went to see our friend Max perform a stand-up act. Then we took his sister out for ice cream, drove her home, and went back to my house. Dante had, like, two beers, I didn't drink at all, there was no drama, no VIP room, no celebrity crap whatsoever. And I don't think I've ever been happier."

"That sounds like a lovely evening," Dr. Parker said.

"We had sex four times," Vanity blurted, covering her face with her hands in a moment of girlish embarrassment.

Dr. Parker chuckled. "Even lovelier."

"I've never connected this way before," Vanity gushed. "It's so pure. It's so honest. I feel sexy and desired and cherished. For the first time, I don't feel like a slut."

Dr. Parker nodded seriously. "I don't mean to temper your feelings, Vanity, because these are wonderful feelings to have. But . . ."

beautiful disaster   141

She waited expectantly for the insight, casting a nervous glance on the coffee table, where a hardcover edition of Aleda Shirley's *Dark Familiar* sat perched on the edge.

"You're just coming out on the other side of a very traumatic episode with J.J. Obviously, Dante is a significant part of that, because he rescued you."

"It's not about that," Vanity argued, a bit too desperately. "This is real."

Dr. Parker shook her head. "I'm not saying that it isn't. My concern is that you remain open to analyzing these feelings. I think your progress is remarkable. You bounced back from a horrific event with great courage and maturity. I've never heard you speak so strongly about yourself in any other session. Frankly, I'm delighted to sit here, listen, and realize that you like yourself. But I'm not comfortable with so much of this being enjoined with Dante. What if things don't work out with him?"

Vanity refused to answer.

"It's not my intention to play Dr. Doomsday here, but let's be realistic. You're seventeen. There will be other relationships. The next guy who comes along might take one look at your 'monster' and say, 'I'm out of here.' What happens then? Will you internalize that and feel unworthy of love all over again?"

Vanity shook her head. "I can't think about this ending. I just want to be happy for once."

Dr. Parker leaned forward. "I want that for you, too. But you must understand something. For this relationship to be as real as you say, then it should be *adding* to your sense of happiness, not *embodying* it."

Vanity fought against the instinct to leave. She had arrived feeling so certain. But difficult questions were beginning to pile up. And the answers rolling around in her mind were too painful to comprehend.

Deep down, Vanity knew exactly what she had to do.

"QUAN!"

Max, startled by the booming, hurried voice of indeterminate gender, hesitated for a microsecond. "I'm trying to reach Keiko Nakamura. Does she work out of this location?"

"Honey, this is the *only* location. And not for long, either. Phones get cut off tomorrow. I think Miss Keiko's packing up her shit. Please remain on the line, sweet clueless one."

"Bitchy queen," Max muttered, just as the hold music commenced with Cher's comeback anthem, "Believe." He listened all the way through to the bridge, and then the ear candy abruptly stopped.

"This is Keiko." She sounded tired, stressed, and miserable.

"Keiko, it's Max Biaggi."

An edgy silence boomed.

"I'm calling from Miami about Christina."

There was a pregnant pause. "What about her?"

Max ignored the hostile tone. "Have you talked with her recently?"

"Why?"

"Because she's missing."

Keiko's voice softened. "For how long?"

"A week or so. I think her mother checked her into an antigay treatment center. Possibly one in Mississippi."

More silence. This time it stretched on and on.

"Are you there?" Max asked.

"Yes," Keiko whispered.

"I need your help finding her."

Keiko sighed. "I can't. I'm sorry."

"You have to take some responsibility for driving that crazy right-wing bitch to do something like this!" Max shouted.

"There's nothing I can do."

Max was fuming. "What do you mean, there's nothing you can do? Have you forgotten the name of your fucked-up organization?"

"QUAN! doesn't exist anymore," Keiko replied bitterly. "We lost a major challenge grant. The board decided to shut us down. If I could help Christina, I would. Honestly. But our offices are closing, and I'm out of a job."

Max made his next decision in the span of a heartbeat. "Not anymore. Get back to work. I'm your new funding source."

Keiko paused a beat. "You're kidding."

"How much will it cost to keep the doors open?"

She hesitated.

"How much, Keiko? I'm not fucking around!"

"At least a hundred thousand."

Max didn't flinch. "Done. I'll have it sent by wire transfer. Just get me the banking details."

"You're serious," Keiko murmured, her voice a mixture of gratitude and awe.

"Yes," Max told her. "And since I'm bankrolling this operation, I want to see some queers uniting for action right now to find Christina Perez."

From: Vanity

I've seen the news. Call me.
I'm here if you need to talk.

6:11 pm 4/24/06

chapter eleven

Vanity knew the story would become an instant media monster. It had everything—celebrity, sex, drugs, crime, and politics. The perfect bouillabaisse for a delicious scandal.

Sipping a hot mug of Asian jasmine white tea, she read the latest online account from the Miami Herald: *"Angry Police, Embattled D.A. Square off in Strip Club Raid, Biaggi Gets Star Treatment After Arrest"*

> The gloves are still off between Miami police and District Attorney Jennifer Velasquez. This time the feud is over the D.A.'s refusal to prosecute five women arrested on prostitution and indecent-exposure charges during yesterday's raid at adult entertainment venue Cheetah.

"These cops were all too eager to arrest the women while turning a blind eye to the alleged johns," Velasquez said. "The real crime here is that five dancers were arrested, booked, and jailed in the same raid that saw Hollywood superstar Max Biaggi be released without charges. It makes you wonder: Was it his stunt double at the club? In the future, I encourage our police department to fight more serious crimes."

Calls to Biaggi's production office were not returned. His official spokesperson also declined comment for this story. Max Biaggi is considered one of cinema's most bankable leading men. His most recent films include *Hijack* and *Hijack II*, for which he commanded a twenty-five-million-dollar salary plus a percentage of gross box office receipts, a deal that reportedly earned the actor more than one hundred million dollars in 2005.

Vanity stopped reading, turning her attention to the blaring television. *Entertainment Tonight* was all over the story. She channel surfed, only to find identical coverage on *Extra*, *E! News*, and *Access Hollywood*.

Every program seemed to be broadcasting the same amateur video footage, which depicted police directing a handcuffed Max Biaggi and Pippa Keith into a waiting paddy wagon.

Vanity's cellular jingled.

It was Dante.

She stretched out to grab the remote control, quickly muting the sound. "Hey, are you watching this?"

"It's on every freaking channel," Dante said. "Turn on CNN. You won't believe this."

Vanity zapped it on and reactivated the audio.

A brittle blonde filled the screen. She looked hard, used up, and mad as hell at every jerkoff in the free world. The TeleType identified her as Raquel "Hellcat" Betts.

"That girl might've been underage in the eyes of the law, but she was all grown up at Cheetah. Called herself Star Baby." The woman sneered, taking a quick drag of a cigarette. "Oh, Miss Underage 'Star Baby' spent lots of private time upstairs with *Max Biaggi*. They went out on a date, too. He took her on his private plane. She walked around here thinking she was God's gift and that the story was going to end up just like *Pretty Woman*. But she's not Julia Roberts. And this isn't Hollywood. Stupid *beep*."

When the report shifted focus to the larger issue of underage strippers across the country, Vanity shut off the audio again. "Have you talked to Max?"

"I've tried several times, but it goes straight to voicemail," Dante said. "This is so fucked up. Like Max needed another reason to hate his father."

Vanity rolled onto her back and stared at her bedroom ceiling, attempting to process the crazy situation. "You know, I think he had strong feelings for Pippa. Max can be so glib about everything. But at the end of the day, he really does care deeply for the people in his inner circle."

"I can't believe she did this to him."

Vanity hesitated. "Let's not judge her. We don't have all the facts."

"Did we watch the same interview just a minute ago?"

"Who knows what that woman's agenda is? She'd probably say Pippa entertained Saudi princes if you just promised her another cigarette."

"Hell, maybe Pippa did."

"Dante, I'm not choosing sides in this. I don't think you should, either."

"Let's just drop it," he said tightly.

Vanity fell silent for one long, frustrated second. "It's not that I don't want to talk about it. I do. I just don't want to get into a game of Pippa bashing. That's all."

"Maybe it's the guy in me, but I'm more concerned about Max. Pippa's true colors are showing. She's a gold digger. The son of a movie star wasn't good enough, so she went straight for the movie star."

Vanity rose up in furious protest, hardly believing that Dante could say those words. "She was working in a strip club! If anything, Max's father probably found *her*!"

"Who cares which way it happened? It's still some low-down shit. And now that everybody knows what Pippa is, all that Prada, Gucci, and Vuitton won't be looking so classy anymore."

"And what is she, Dante? Please share."

He hesitated. "I think it's obvious."

"How can you turn on her so quickly? You don't even know the circumstances that pushed her into a job like that."

"You're right." His tone mocked her. "Maybe she was stripping to pay for her grandmother's surgery."

"God!" Vanity shrieked. "You're such an asshole!" She came close to hanging up. But in the end, she just hung on the line, silently raging.

Dante sighed. "Let's not snipe at each other," he said quietly. "This thing has nothing to do with us."

Vanity could feel that nagging impulse to keep fighting even when you know an argument is over. She touched the neat, white bandage dressed around her upper arm. The sutures had been removed a few days ago. Though healing, the knife wound was still tender.

"I'm sorry . . . for sounding off," Dante said. "Really. And I'm not just saying that for the make-up sex." He laughed a little. "Maybe this is one of those Mars and Venus things."

"Yeah, maybe so."

His voice dropped an octave. "If you're still pissed, feel free to take it out on me in bed."

Something stirred inside her—an aching physical need to be with him. Slowly, it began to undo her resolve. But Vanity managed to shake off the hunger.

"Do you want me to come over?"

"My father's home," Vanity said. She was lying. Simon St. John had left for New York that morning.

"Damn. I thought you said he'd only be in town for one night."

"I did. He changed his trip to later in the week."

"That sucks. I've gotten spoiled waking up with you the last several days."

"I know," Vanity murmured. "Me, too."

"We could always go to a hotel," Dante suggested. "Even if it's just for a few hours. I've already got symptoms of withdrawal."

"It's tempting . . . but . . . I feel like I should go see Pippa."

Dante let out a horny groan. "How am I supposed to sleep tonight?"

"I don't know." She paused a beat, then added silkily, "Why don't you try your right hand and an Ambien."

"Oh, that was cold, baby," Dante replied with good humor. "That was cold."

Vanity grinned, feeling guilty about the lie, but not guilty enough to reverse it.

"Call and let me know how it goes. I'll do the same if I catch up with Max."

"Okay."

"I'll miss you."

Vanity signed off, quietly devastated, her heart pounding as tiny fragments of doubt began to overwhelm her. She sat there on the edge of the bed, both arms wrapped tightly around her stomach, thinking about the last session with Dr. Parker. She had an important decision to make about Dante. An hour passed, and then another.

But she was still no closer to a resolution.

Pippa took a step backward to analyze the clothing spread across the bed and floor in tidy little piles. At first glance, it looked as if the roof had collapsed and Neiman Marcus had fallen in.

Gucci, Prada, Fendi, Stella McCartney, Alexander McQueen, Chloe, Zac Posen, Tory Burch, Marc Jacobs, Valentino, Jean Paul Gaultier, Christian Dior, and Escada.

The sheer volume of the collection stunned Pippa. It made the task of packing up to move quite daunting. For a fleeting moment, she secretly fantasized about tossing the bare essentials into a lovely bag, boarding a plane, and never turning back. But the moment passed. No way was she leaving her fashion treasures behind.

Suddenly, Pippa started to shake. Oh God, if she started crying, then she might never stop. Somehow she managed to keep the tears at bay. Her body felt like lead.

Her mind felt like mush. It was sheer overstimulation and exhaustion.

For the last thirty-six hours, Pippa had not slept so much as a nanosecond. But she plunged forward with a fiery will, seeking strength from her deep commitment to get the hell out of Miami as fast as possible.

Three Louis Vuitton steamer trunks were already half full. Glancing around at what remained, Pippa surmised that she just might have enough room for everything, including her beauty products, of which she had loads—La Prairie, Chanel, Guerlain, and SK-II among the pricey lot.

The trunk set had been a scrumptious eBay find that drained twenty thousand dollars from Pippa's Cheetah kitty. It was worth the extravagance, though. The vintage pieces were *ages* old and, evidenced by the travel stickers affixed on all sides, had seen many transcontinental adventures in exotic places like Shanghai, Constantinople, Yokohama, and Jerusalem.

A hint of a grin crept onto Pippa's lips as she realized that her poor trunks would probably be bored rigid on their next trip, which was only to New York. Ha! Paris sometime soon, dearest ones, promise.

Pippa had no friends in Manhattan, no contacts to speak of, and no plan in place upon arrival. But she also had no worries. After all, as the legend went, Madonna, with only thirty-five dollars in her pocket, had moved to the city and commanded a taxi driver to just leave her in the middle of Times Square. Life had sorted out bloody well good for her.

The doorbell chimed.

Pippa experienced a sudden, white-hot fear. She crept to the window and peeked out into the black night, startled to see Vanity's Spyker C8 Laviolette parked on the street. But it was a far better discovery than Vinnie's Lincoln Navigator SUV, which is exactly what she feared to see most.

She breathed out a sigh of relief . . . for the moment. Last night's voicemail rage from Vinnie had gripped her in a constant state of paranoia. It took no effort to recall the sick bastard's words verbatim.

"I hope you fucking rot in hell! You lying, deceitful little cunt! That underage bullshit scheme of yours is causing me big trouble! If I ever see you again, I'll make you pay with blood, teeth, and bones, bitch!"

Pippa tried to shake off the horrifying sense memory and moved quickly to intercept Vanity. She opened the door no wider than twelve inches.

"May I come in?" Vanity asked.

Pippa shook her head. "Now's not a good time."

But Vanity was undeterred. "I won't stay long."

Reluctantly, Pippa allowed her entry.

Vanity stepped inside and surveyed the modest surroundings. "This is the first time I've been to your house."

Pippa rolled her eyes. "Forgive the mess. Our South Beach condo is being remodeled."

Vanity's gaze tracked down the short hallway. With Pippa's bedroom door wide open, evidence of a major packing project was in plain sight. "Going somewhere?"

"Yes," Pippa said tightly. "Far away from here." She bounded back to her private hovel and proceeded to continue with her work.

Vanity followed. "What about school?"

"What about it?" Pippa snapped.

"Graduation is only a month away."

"It's not like I'm going to college."

"You don't need to run away, Pippa. Take it from someone who knows. Things are never quite as bad as you think they are."

"And sometimes they're worse," Pippa countered, throwing a folded stack of Juicy Couture separates into the nearest trunk.

Vanity stood there, momentarily speechless, taking in the enormity of Pippa's designer inventory. "You bitch. You've got more clothes than I do." She picked up and inspected an Anna Sui top. "Nicer ones, too!"

Pippa cracked a smile and playfully snatched the garment from Vanity's hands. "And I earned every thread and stitch."

"Oh, I bet you did."

Pippa glared at Vanity.

Vanity glared back at Pippa.

And then the two girls fell into a brief fit of laughter. When it ended, there was an awkward silence.

Finally, Pippa broke it. "I should finish packing."

"Would you like some help?"

Pippa shrugged carelessly. But deep down she was grateful for Vanity's visit. Save for Vinnie's vicious rant, her mobile had only rung once in the last two days. And that had been her mum checking in from her latest promotional stop outside Atlanta, where she was booked for a week-long demonstration at the Mall of Georgia.

It seemed logical that Sophie might blissfully escape the scandal. Pippa's status as a minor had kept her name out of the press, and unless her mum had been squatting in front of the telly to absorb every minute of the day's entertainment news programs, the sordid facts might just slip past her. After all, the next news cycle could very well wipe the mess clean. Honestly. How long could they blather on about one star's strip club visit?

"Have you spoken to Max?" Vanity asked.

Pippa sighed. "He and I were pretty much on our last conversation at the Improv. I don't think recent events will do anything to open a dialogue."

Vanity busied herself with the job of piling multiple

boxes of Manolo Blahnik shoes into one of the trunks. "So where are you going?"

"New York."

"To do what?"

"I'm not sure. I've always wanted to be a Rockette. Maybe I'll do that."

"Really? That sounds cool."

"When I was a little girl, our family spent a Christmas in New York once. My mum went shopping, and my father took me on a date to Radio City Music Hall to see them." Enchanted by the memory, Pippa dreamily sat down on the edge of the bed. "I remember being in awe of how glamorous they were. Those perfect kick lines. That precisely timed fall during the wooden soldier routine. It was so magical." One beat. "And one of the few positive things I can recollect about my snot rag of a father."

Vanity tilted her head. "That's funny. When I was little, my father took me to see the Rockettes, too. It's one of my favorite times with him." Suddenly, a mischievous smile brightened her face. "Can you actually do one of their kicks?"

"Please." Pippa sniffed haughtily, as if she were being asked to count to three. She stood up and unleashed an impressive eye-level kick.

Vanity screamed. "If I tried to do that, I would totally fall on my ass and probably pull my hamstring, too!"

Pippa giggled. "At peak season, those girls do five shows a day. That means fifteen hundred of those kicks in a single day."

"Do another one," Vanity said.

Pippa smiled and let it rip, delivering another perfect high-flyer.

Vanity clapped with delight. "You know, I never told you how amazing you were in *Sweet Charity*."

"Thanks," Pippa said quietly. "God, that seems like so long ago."

"For me, too." Vanity gave her an earnest look. "You could star on Broadway. You're that good."

"Oh, I know." Pippa grinned. "And I'd like to do that one day. But first I want to disappear, in a sense. I don't want to be in the spotlight. That's why the idea of being a Rockette is so appealing. I'd just be one of the girls wearing the same red lipstick, the same false eyelashes, and the same sexy costume." She rolled her eyes. "And the best part? No fat, ugly wankers would have a chance to pinch my ass! Even if they paid top dollar for an orchestra seat!"

Vanity began to laugh, though it faded as she looked searchingly into Pippa's eyes.

It was impossible to ignore the elephant in the room any longer, especially since it was wearing a thong and dancing to that ghastly Europe single from the wretched eighties, "The Final Countdown."

Pippa struggled to close the lid on the first trunk that was full to bursting, then sat down on top of it, suddenly quiet and moody. She glanced up at Vanity. "So sorry to leave like this and steal your scandal-queen thunder."

Vanity sank onto the floor and leaned against the bed, a wry grin on her beautiful face. "Please. You're an amateur."

Pippa took in a deep breath. What a soddy mess her life had become.

Vanity saw her opening and went for it. "How did everything get to this point?"

Pippa braced herself for the confessional. Instinctively, she knew that it would be emotionally cleansing. "One night last summer, Max took me to Mynt. I got trashed and danced on the bar and some guy slipped me a hundred-dollar bill." She shrugged. "I was hooked. I mean, after that, the idea of stocking cheap denim at Old Navy for minimum wage hardly seemed like an option. I needed . . . I *wanted* to make a lot of money. So I showed up at Cheetah with one of Max's brilliant fake IDs, and I got hired right away."

Vanity listened intently, not even a hint of judgment in her eyes. "It was that simple?"

Pippa nodded. "Getting the job was. My first time on the stage was awful, but somehow my body just sputtered to life and started moving to the music. And after the song ended, guys threw cash at me. Most of them were pathetic and vile, but when you're counting up your take at the end of the night, a pig's twenty-dollar bill is the same as a hot stockbroker's. So it's, like, whatever."

Vanity sighed, shaking her head, as if in awe. "How did you do it? I can't imagine. I've struggled with the objectification of certain modeling assignments. But to take off your clothes in front of . . ."

"It's all about money," Pippa said matter-of-factly. "Not having it can push you through all sorts of humiliations on your way to getting it. I remember first moving here. You had the most amazing clothes, and I felt like some street urchin by comparison. I had, like, one or two nice things that I wore to tatters. Max would take me to all these amazing clubs, and I couldn't afford to buy one bloody drink. It was awful. I wanted to be the glamour girl again, and I didn't care what I had to do to make that happen. So off went the clothes."

Vanity was silent.

Pippa continued. "It's strange. Sometimes I would feel this powerful rush, you know? Like I was a huntress at the top of my game. I could pick out a guy." She snapped her fingers. "Like that. The vulnerable ones were easy to spot. They were so desperate to hang out with a naked girl. But you know, it was still objectification, no matter how much I thought I was in control. I could be listening to them drone on about their boring jobs and their fat wives, but even in the losers' eyes, I was nothing more than tits and ass. And some of the others would just look right through me and say the most disgusting shit. It changed me. It hardened me. I became this cold cash-making machine. And I couldn't stop. I needed to strip for the money to buy expensive things. But then I needed the high from the shopping fix to help me deal with the fact that I was stripping."

"A vicious circle," Vanity remarked.

"Yeah, *exactly*," Pippa said. "Vicious as hell. Getting arrested was probably a good thing. But it was a bullshit charge. Some drunk frat boy ripped off my thong during the raid. When I told the police that I was attacked, they just laughed. Then they turned around and let the creep go. So much for American justice. As long as you're rich, white, and swinging a few balls, you can get away with anything." She covered her face in her hands, overcome with emotion, but the moment passed. She breathed deeply, running her fingers through her hair.

"I saw the interview with that dancer from the club," Vanity began, probing gingerly. "Those things she said about you and Max's father . . ."

"He's a sick bastard!" Pippa shouted. "I'd love nothing more than to see him trapped in the North Pole with his pants down! That way he'd get severe frostbite on his dick, and they'd have to amputate!"

Vanity's eyes widened in alarm.

Pippa thundered on. "He requested me for the private room several times. In the beginning, he was sweet and tender. All he wanted to do was suck my toes."

Vanity's mouth dropped open.

Pippa pulled a face. "At least he was good at it. Anyway, I fell for him in a major way. I'll admit that. I'm just a girl with a lousy father. He's an older, handsome movie star. What else do you expect? But then he got me on his private plane. That's when he turned into a crazy monster. He called me a whore and tried to rape me."

"Oh my God!" Vanity exclaimed.

Pippa stood up and peeled off her cashmere hoodie, leaving her in a white cotton tank. The bruises on her wrists and arms were still clearly visible.

Vanity gasped.

"You should've seen them a week ago."

"Pippa, I'm so sorry."

"Yeah, well, *he's* more sorry. The only reason he stopped is because I convinced him I was seventeen and threatened to go straight to the media. Then I blackmailed the motherfucker for a million. No regrets, either. I deserve it."

Vanity shook her head in disbelief. "Are you going to tell Max any of this?"

"Why?" Pippa asked. "So he can laugh about it in his next comedy act?"

"Max wouldn't do that," Vanity maintained. She spoke passionately. "He cares about you, Pippa. But have you actually given him a chance to prove it? You've lied to him about everything. You've avoided him for months. He should know the truth, though."

Pippa shook her head. "I can't face him again. Not after the things we said to each other at the comedy club. And certainly not after this. I look at him, Vanity, and I want to see *my* Max, but all I can see is his goddamn father. That disgusting pig of a man! I've loused up everything! I just want to leave. You know? I just want to leave this place and forget that I ever came here!"

And then Pippa raced into the bathroom and shut the door, sobbing uncontrollably.

Vanity just stood there, heartbroken and helpless, desperate to provide Pippa comfort, but not sure how. Nervously, she rapped softly on the door. "Pippa, I'm not leaving you like this. I'll stay right here until you come out, okay? We'll talk more. I'll help you pack. Anything that you want."

But Pippa's crying only intensified.

Vanity closed her eyes, both hands pressed against the

door, wishing she could find the perfect words to make it better. Finally, she gave voice to a few simple ones. "I'm here, Pippa. You're not alone."

And then she thought about Max. He was a victim in all of this, as well. Where was he? And how was he dealing with it?

From: Max

Revenge sex. Sanctuary. 10 sharp.

8:19 pm 4/24/06

chapter twelve

Max was back at Sanctuary, sexing it up again, already down a few Red Bulls and Levels, feeling no pain, feeling *much* pain.

He loved watching the way his stepmonster's hair swayed back and forth as she balanced herself on the bed and speared him like a carnival freak swallowing a sword.

Max's heart started to pound. This was their third round of the night, and he was enjoying it more than ever. Admitting that only increased his pleasure.

He had never been the kind of guy to go after MILFs. Max much preferred girls closer to his age. But an opportunity to bed down Faith Biaggi, his father's second wife, was just too tempting to pass up.

Max could feel his excitement mounting. With a harsh

cry, he climaxed, writhing with such abandon that he banged his skull against the headboard, the impact so hard that he thought one or both might have cracked. "Oh, shit!"

Faith laughed.

Max rubbed the back of his head, already feeling the beginnings of a knot. Finally, he laughed, too. "I think I gave myself a concussion."

"Should I call your father?" Faith asked. "Maybe he'll rush home to check on his loyal son."

Max looked at his stepmonster with something close to amazement. She seemed to be enjoying this sweet act of revenge more than he was.

Faith slid off the mattress and sashayed, gloriously naked, over to the stereo. In seconds, the romantic sounds of Michael Bublé came lilting from the speakers. "This is your father's favorite music to make love to."

At first, Max thought she was kidding. But Faith was dead serious.

She stopped to light a candle and gave him a bad-girl grin. "You're bigger than he is where it counts."

Max raised his brow. "You would know better than anyone."

"Does that make you happy?"

"Would it make him unhappy?"

"Absolutely," Faith trilled.

Max sighed. "Then hell yes it makes me happy."

Faith straddled him, planting her aerobic thighs against Max's slim hips, the weight and sensation of her body so wildly erotic.

The scent of tuberose wafted in the air.

Her approach this time was more seductive than ever before, an intoxicating orgy of hands and fingers, lips and tongue.

But no matter the sexual distractions, his mind remained on a single track: Max Biaggi and Pippa Keith. It was the ultimate betrayal. The only girl who had ever told him no and his own father. Christ. Max would rather have learned about Pippa being with *anyone* else. Even an entire football team, for that matter.

The revelations had rocked the Star Island mansion. His stepmonster was too weak to leave the son of a bitch, so the twit just drank more. And tonight she had been just loaded enough to take him up on his nasty little offer of sexual justice.

Max guessed the marriage might endure a few more months, end of the year at best. His father would divorce her, enforce the prenuptial agreement, and then Faith would spend the rest of her life hating him.

Shoshanna had weighed in as only she knew how. "Okay, *ewww*! Daddy gets arrested in a strip club, and some skanky woman is on TV saying he's into underage girls! Why does everything always happen to me?"

Of course, the tabloid man of the moment had chosen to avoid all of them. Fucking coward. Following the arrest, he immediately jetted to Los Angeles to huddle with a public relations crisis team.

Suddenly, Max let out a soft, involuntary moan as the sensation of Faith's tongue licking his armpit sent shivers down his body. "How many times are we going to do this?" Max asked.

"Give it to me one more time and you break his record. Even when he's pumped up with Viagra."

"I like the sound of that," Max admitted.

"I thought you would," Faith said.

Max's mind tripped off into space. Graduation was a month away, and he was still undecided about college, making the rest of his life one big question mark. A change of venue sounded exciting. Maybe Los Angeles. He could check out the local comedy scene, find a new group to hang with, start a whole new routine.

Faith reached down to smooth a hand along Max's cheek, then left it there. "I can't get over how much you look like him." She grinned sadly.

Shit. The last thing he needed was for this woman to turn into some kind of emotional nutcase.

Faith let her hand slide down Max's neck. It came to rest against the hollow of his throat. "What do you think he would do if he ever found us together like this?"

Max stared back at her for a long, thoughtful second. "I think he would divorce you, disinherit me, and then kill us both."

"Do you really think it would make him that crazy?" she asked. Her tone implied that a resounding "yes" would be the preferred answer.

"Yeah, I do," Max told her.

"Just knowing that will get me through the bad times," Faith murmured, her hand leaving Max's neck and skating all the way down to check his state of readiness.

Max smiled. He was all systems go.

"One more time," Faith breathed.

It was such a sick little twist. Max Biaggi getting his son's best girl. Max Biaggi Jr. taking his father's second wife.

If the bastard knew what was happening here, then he would go mad. The words being said. The fantasies being played out. The comparisons being made. It would murder his father's ego. And the awareness of that propelled Max to finish off the night like a champ.

He pushed Faith down onto the bed and kissed her hungrily, his mouth rough and demanding, his biceps straining to pull her closer.

"Who's better in bed?" Max asked. He wanted to hear her say it out loud.

"You are," Faith whispered.

Max's Sidekick II vibrated.

He started to ignore the call. But then he changed his mind. Reluctantly, he disengaged from Faith and stretched out to check the tiny screen.

It was Keiko.

Christina. Max felt his stomach lurch. He snatched the device and answered with a breathless, "What's up?"

"I know where she is," Keiko said.

Christina lay immobile in the dark, hoping, listening, and waiting.

Sometimes she felt like being cut off from everything and everyone was driving her insane. At this point, her mind had become a bad neighborhood that even she should avoid.

One moment she would fantasize about ending her life in the bloodiest of ways—to escape the pain, to end the fight, and to inflict as much guilt as possible on her mother.

And in the very next instant she would build elaborate scenes about breaking out with revolutionary fanfare—to stage protests, to speak out against intolerance, and to cause enough public chaos to derail the campaign of the hopeful Senator Paulina Perez.

According to the first day's orientation session, over which the esteemed Pastor Chet Hobbs presided,

Christina and the others had been dispatched to Salvation Pointe for "a health intervention that would instill emotional, physical, spiritual, and moral cleansings." Perhaps that made for good copy on the glossy brochure, but in practice, there was no evidence here of anything resembling "health."

The sadistic irony was that Christina had never been more *un*healthy. She rarely ate. She hardly slept. She lost weight. She developed acne. She stayed up nights sobbing. She questioned whether anyone loved her. She obsessed over meaningless things.

There was some comfort to be found in the interaction with other residents—people like Zack, who had become a certain lifeline—but she still missed her friends desperately. Christina spoke to them in her head all the time, imagining conversations. She longed to see Vanity's gorgeous face, to hear Max call her "Jap," to get a warm hug from Dante, and to decode Pippa's loopy British slang.

The silence at Salvation Pointe at times made her feel crazy, and the harsh restrictions pushed it toward total madness. Christina felt as if the world had stopped altogether. Was life inside this compound all that there was and all that there ever would be? Sometimes she believed the answer was yes.

Here she was, endless days into her course of "treatment," starving for anything that might loosen the mental straitjacket—a favorite song, a movie, the sound of a voice from the outside, a magazine, a newspaper, even a goddamn sketch pad! The fascists at Salvation Pointe forbade her to draw, dismissing it as a "boy's hobby" and telling her that a girl should learn how to cook. It was unspeakable.

Christina had to get away from this place. With each passing hour, she could feel herself inching closer and closer to the edge of a psychotic break. The claustrophobia of this tiny world and the monotony of her own thoughts were taking a brutal toll. She needed outlets to get through her worst moments, even if it was just sobering world news to remind her that circumstances could be far more damning elsewhere.

In answer, Christina's memory recalled a horrific story about the Sudan and the genocide in Darfur. There was a place called Kalma camp, where untold thousands squatted after being driven from burned villages. The women faced daily risk of gang rape, and those who suffered attacks were ostracized for life and forced to build their own huts. So if a Sudanese girl could soldier on in those conditions, then Christina could certainly get through her problems at Salvation Pointe.

Suddenly, there was a high-pitched scream and the sound of breaking glass.

But Christina was hardly alarmed. She bolted from the bed, a grateful smile on her face as she dashed to the door, cracking it just a sliver to peer out.

Somebody give Richie the Golden Globe for Best Actress. He *was* every bit as good as Scarlett Johansson.

The night monitors were in a dither, trying to placate Richie during his fake panic attack *and* order the worried residents spilling into the corridor back to their rooms.

Zack's plan had worked perfectly.

Christina slipped away unnoticed and made a beeline for her secret destination, located on the far end of the building. She moved fast and breathed deeply. It was the closest air to freedom she had known since arriving here.

She darted past the cafeteria, group therapy room, Bible study hall, and activity center, everything blacker than night and tomblike still.

And then Christina saw it . . . at the end of a darkened hall . . . a door ajar . . . a beam of light pouring out . . . Chet Hobbs's private office.

She approached slowly, stealthily peeking inside to be sure it was empty. Yes, thank God. With great relief, she crept into the outer room and slipped behind the massive mahogany desk.

Christina's heart raced. She sat in front of the idle iMac, the screen blank, its power light fading in and out like a distress signal. All it took to wake up the computer was a mere touch of the keyboard's space bar. But would the back-to-life chime give her away?

Frightful and uncertain, she reached for the telephone, one of those complicated multiline office beasts. Establishing an outside line required several nervous attempts. Finally, Christina got lucky by punching eight and waiting for a dial tone. But her joy crashed soon after. The system would not allow her to make a long-distance call.

All of a sudden, Christina froze, the low murmur of voices stopping her cold.

The sounds were coming from the adjacent room, its door closed, a soft ray of light visible underneath.

Christina listened acutely, picking up the faint sound of crying. The discovery unnerved her. It could only be Zack, here for his private counseling with Chet Hobbs.

She tiptoed over and pressed her ear against the door.

"Your father thinks you're a queer. That's why he sent you to Salvation Pointe." Chet Hobbs was talking.

Christina's stomach dropped fast.

"Are you a queer?" Hobbs asked.

"I don't know." Zack's tears muffled his answer.

Christina just stood there, mortified.

"It's okay, Zack. A lot of boys come to Salvation Pointe confused just like you. But it's important to identify a problem before you try to solve it. I happen to have a very special way of helping boys find out if they're queer or not. And after we establish that, the healing can begin. Does that sound like a good plan?"

Zack continued to cry.

A sick feeling swamped over Christina. It was intense,

all-consuming, and came close to buckling her knees. Refusing to eat. Going without sleep. The extremities of this nightmare were tearing her apart. She fought for strength.

From inside the room, there was the *clink* of a belt being unfastened and then the sound of a zipper going down.

"I want you to suck my dick, Zack. I can always tell if a boy's queer by the way his mouth takes to a hard dick."

Christina felt an instant cold sweat slick her body. Was this a crazy mind playing tricks? Had she gone insane? Because how could Salvation Point be this depraved? It was beyond the ken of any reality.

She stumbled back to the outer office, feeling weaker than ever, dizzy even, almost faint. But she had to reach the computer and send out an email. For some reason, she thought of Max first. Maybe because he had the most resources. All she had to do was tell him where she was and what was going on. Max would find a way to help her.

As the room began to spin, Christina lost her balance. She steadied herself against the desk, allowing time for the spell to pass. But the horrible feeling seemed to linger forever. She weaved into the corridor, living on the desperate hope that a splash of water from the fountain would set her right.

"What are you doing all the way down here?"

Startled, Christina turned to see a figure upon her. But

before she could implore the night monitor to help Zack, her last bit of strength evaporated. Everything turned to black as she slumped into the woman's arms.

When Christina woke up the next morning, the moments leading up to her fainting haunted her with crystal clarity. At first, she thought it might be one of those riveting, hallucinogenic nightmares that attack the mind when the body is in severe distress.

But an eerie sensation that something terrible had happened came over her. The air was humid with it. She raced across the hall to Zack's room.

What she saw next would change Christina for the rest of her life. It was an image that she would never forget. And it was a way out that she would never again consider.

She saw Zack Webber with his wrists sliced open, lying in a pool of his own blood.

From: Keiko

Everything is in place. Let's rock.

9:47 am 4/25/06

chapter thirteen

he Cessna Citation Bravo approached a private airstrip in Madison, Mississippi.

From his pedestal-mounted ivory leather-upholstered swivel chair, Max had spent most of the flight in cellular conference with Keiko.

If he knew one thing about the sushi bitch, it was this: She gave good activism. Within hours of discovering Christina's whereabouts, Keiko had cobbled together a grassroots protest to rival the immigration demonstrations. She had also compiled a revealing dossier on Pastor Chet Hobbs, the director of Salvation Pointe and CEO of Holy Waters, a megachurch with a congregation boasting over three thousand members.

Max scrolled through the information on his Sidekick

II. On paper, Chet Hobbs appeared to be the Stepford religious leader. He was in his mid-thirties with charismatic good looks, a pretty wife, three adorable children, and the proper credentials from Bob Jones University.

Hobbs had scaled the ranks of the Jesus-as-business-model world high and fast, commandeering his own place of worship at a young age and making a name for himself with a big entertainment style. His sermons featured large projection screens, a twelve-piece stage band, and were routinely overseen by a lighting designer.

Salvation Pointe, now in its fourth year of operations and bringing in an average of three million dollars per year, had been Hobbs's dream project, going from napkin brainstorm sketch to ribbon-cutting ceremony within two years. And already it was widely considered *the* market leader in the controversial gay-prevention program industry.

"This shit is un-freaking-believable!" Max exclaimed, glancing up to engage Vanity and Dante, who sat opposite him on the chartered plane. "It says here that since Salvation Pointe opened its doors in 2002, there have been *three* onsite suicides."

Vanity gasped. "Oh my God."

"How can they still be in operation?" Dante asked.

"State and federal authorities don't provide much oversight because it's religious-based," Max explained, his nimble fingers working fast on the device. "And if the parents are brain-dead enough to send their kid to this kind of place, I'm sure they're too stupid to question what's really going on there."

Vanity grinned, secretly amused by something.

Max did a double take. "What?"

"Nothing . . . I just never imagined that you of all people would become so political," Vanity said, still smiling. Pride shone from her eyes.

"Who, me?" Max asked cockily, gesturing to the one-size-too-small red Che Guevara T-shirt hugging his body and enhancing his biceps. "I'm a rebel, baby."

Dante chuckled. "I think the last thing you campaigned against was MACPA's crackdown on oral sex in the school parking lot."

"At the time it was an important issue," Max insisted lightly. "I was in *my* car on *my* lunch period. For me, it was a matter of basic human rights."

Dante shook his head, laughing. He glanced at Vanity, winked, and reached for her hand.

Max noticed how she avoided Dante's gesture with consummate skill, suddenly checking for something in her eye, even producing an exquisite jeweled compact to prolong and authenticate the moment. This wasn't the same couple from the Improv.

Max gave Vanity a curious look.

She stared back. Her eyes were hard, as if daring him to say a single word.

Max let it go. What choice did he have? Vanity had attempted to talk to him about Pippa, and he'd shut her down fast. Turnabout was fair play.

"So tell us, funny guy, when's your next stand-up shot?" Dante asked.

"I don't know," Max said, somewhat distracted as he gazed out the window, taking in an endless sea of green. "I might check out the scene in L.A. The Comedy Store's there. Plus another Improv location. I could give it a year or more. Stick around for a few pilot seasons. See what happens."

A meaningful silence seized the small cabin.

Suddenly, Max realized that this was the first time one of them had spoken in explicit terms about post-graduation plans. "What about the two of you?"

Vanity glared at him.

Dante shrugged. "Just work on my music." He rolled his eyes. "Of course, if my mother had her way, I'd be enrolling in a trade school."

"Yeah, you could be a cosmetologist or a radiology tech," Max joked. He glanced at Vanity.

She offered nothing.

Screw it. He decided to press her. "Any plans for the rest of your life, sweetheart?"

"I'm more concerned about what's going to happen in the next thirty minutes," Vanity said.

The Cessna had already started its descent. In the distance, Max could make out a private airstrip. He downed what remained of his cranberry juice and prepared for landing.

"Pippa's moving to New York," Vanity announced. "She wants to be a Rockette."

Max made eye contact with Dante. "Your girlfriend must have me confused with someone who gives a shit."

Dante gave Vanity a look that suggested she might consider backing off.

The plane scaled the tops of trees, the wheels trundled down, and within minutes, the aircraft hit solid ground.

"Your father tried to rape her," Vanity said acidly. "Do you give a shit about that?"

Max was stunned. For several long, tense seconds he said nothing. "Is that what she told you?"

Vanity nodded severely. "And I saw the bruises. It happened on his private plane. The same night we were in New York at Tar Beach."

The pilot killed the engines.

Max sat there, gripping the armrests, fighting for calm, putting it all together. He knew it was true. Instinctively, he just knew. So that was the reason why his father had been unreachable on the night Shoshanna had been fighting for her life. Because the bastard was forcing himself on Pippa. And then he had the gall to show up the next day at the hospital, play concerned papa for the paparazzi, and blame Max for everything.

If you weren't so busy prancing around like some party-planning faggot, this never would've happened! Max Biaggi had roared.

Vanity unbuckled her safety harness and leaned forward, touching Max's knee with her fingertips. "I know this is awful. But you have to know the truth. Pippa got caught up in a bad situation. It can't end this way, Max. Not for the two of you. And not for the rest of us, either." Tears welled in her eyes. "There's a reason I don't want to think about the future. It's because I'm afraid of what it will be without all of us together. We're the fabulous five, right?"

Max nodded, touching her hand.

"I've been such a fucking mess that I've missed almost everything. But sometimes I feel like I got through it all because of the connections. You know? We're connected. Even in spirit, there's something special about all of us as a group. We've got a month before graduation. We can put it all together, Max. We deserve to make it the best time ever."

Max touched his beautiful friend's face. Gently, he rubbed out a rolling tear with his thumb. And then he laughed a little.

"What?" Vanity asked, almost hurt.

"Nothing . . . I just never imagined that you of all people would become so sentimental." He smiled.

She smiled back.

"When does Pippa leave?"

"Tonight."

Max nodded. "Don't worry. I'll make it right." He cradled Vanity's cheek in one hand and reached out to bump Dante's fist with his other. "We're still four strong. But one member's down." He paused a beat. "Let's go save Jap."

Mere hours after the discovery of Zack's body, it was business as usual at Salvation Pointe. The residents were back on schedule.

Christina, in a near catatonic state, made the walking trail around the man-made lake in a zombielike daze. She could barely put one leg in front of the other.

Jordan and Richie flanked her in a show of solidarity, as the three of them had been closest to Zack.

"I shouldn't have broken the window," Richie said, his voice full of guilt and remorse. "They said that's how he did it. He found a shard of glass they missed in the cleanup. It's my fault."

"Stop saying that," Jordan said. "You're torturing yourself for no reason. If Zack hadn't found that shard of glass, he would've broken his own window to get one."

Richie expelled a deep sigh. "I still can't believe it. He seemed so happy yesterday. Well, you know, by Salvation Pointe standards, at least. He just never struck me as the suicidal type."

All of a sudden, Christina stopped. It was a gorgeous Mississippi spring day, the sun shining, the sky brilliant blue, the fragrant scent of honeysuckle in the air.

She admired the landscaping. The grounds were lovingly attended. Every blade of grass, every flower, every shrub, every tree was botanical garden perfect.

So how could there be so much ugliness here?

Up ahead, the team leader in charge of the walk halted and gestured for everyone to catch up, ostensibly to hear an important announcement. "Let's go . . . let's go," he called out.

Christina cut her eyes at him savagely. Impatient prick.

His security badge pronounced him Chad K, and he was a notorious joke among the residents, with his smug attitude, color-treated dark hair, and big, white teeth. The story had gone round and round about his discharge from the marines for appearing on a military-themed sex site.

Just days after his wife had given birth to their third child, Chad K was shooting a load for the camera while a paratrooper stood over him. But he was cured now, having gone through Pastor Hobbs's one-on-one "Soul Salvation" course.

"Attention!" Chad K shouted. "There's been a minor change to today's schedule. I'm sure everyone is upset about this morning's tragedy. It's a terrible loss. We all loved Zack. Pastor Hobbs will be leading us in prayer at a special assembly as soon as we get back."

For Christina, the outrage was suddenly too much to bear. The sadistic hypocrisy had to stop! But before she could react, all hell broke loose.

A crowd came surging up the circular drive, crammed body to body, a marching colorful sea of YES, I AM! T-shirts, ripped fatigues, and rainbow flags. They were chanting loud and proud, "Being gay is okay . . . being gay is okay. . . ."

At first, Christina could hardly believe her eyes. But then she fixed her gaze and knew for certain. It was Keiko leading the pack of demonstrators!

Christina dashed toward her, leaping off the paved trail and running across the freshly mowed grass, just as Salvation Pointe staff and security began appearing from all directions.

"You're trespassing on private property!" one voice yelled.

"The police are on their way," another voice shouted.

Breathlessly, Christina reached Keiko, embracing her tightly. "Oh my God! How did you know? How did you find me?"

"Max," Keiko said, drawing back to get a better look at Christina. "Are you okay?"

"Yes . . . no . . . I don't know." Christina began to cry.

Keiko hugged her again.

But this time Christina pulled away. "It's awful here, Keiko. A friend of mine committed suicide. I heard him being molested by the director last night. I didn't see anything, but I *heard* it."

Keiko nodded knowingly. "Pastor Hobbs. I've tracked down an ex-resident who's willing to go on record. I'll need to arrange a statement from you, too."

"Of course," Christina agreed. "Anything. Anything at all." She turned, astonished to see a stretch Bentley racing up the drive, followed by two police vehicles, sirens screaming.

"But now you have to get out of here," Keiko said firmly. "Go with Max. He's in the limo. I'll contact you later. They won't get away with this. I swear."

"But they're going to arrest you!" Christina cried.

This made Keiko smile. "These are the moments that I live for."

Two Salvation Pointe staff members were stomping toward Christina, ordering her to separate from the protesters.

"Go!" Keiko screamed.

Christina hesitated. And then she broke out in a mad run for what she knew was quite possibly her life.

The Bentley coasted to a stop, the rear passenger door opened, and Max stepped out, a glorious sight in his Tom Ford sunglasses and Che Guevara T-shirt. He opened his arms.

Christina fell directly into them, sobbing convulsively. Seeing Vanity and Dante inside the cabin, her emotions intensified.

Max kissed her forehead. "Get in, Jap. We're going home."

And then it dawned on Christina that she didn't have a home anymore. This time her mother had gone too far. She needed time and space from Paulina Perez. How much she didn't know. "Where am I supposed to go?"

"You're staying with me at the mansion," Max said easily. "But my family's fucked-up, too, so I can't promise much of a difference."

From: Dante

We need to talk.

8:28 pm 4/25/06

chapter fourteen

He waited for her at Jumbo's, an old dive on Seventh Avenue that had been around for more than fifty years. No attitude. No celebrity buzz. Just kick-ass food.

Dante's new job running errands at Bogart Recording paid decently. But a hot Miami restaurant bill could put "decently" in the grave. So he settled for the nine-dollar Wing-Ding Deal here.

When Vanity arrived, every diner stopped to gawk at the impossibly gorgeous girl. She wore a linen-camouflage-print camisole dress, cinched by a brown leather belt that accentuated her delicious curves.

A waitress swooped in and slammed two sweet teas onto the table. If Vanity hated the place, then she hid her displeasure with kindness, quickly agreeing to a monster plate of fried chicken, onion rings, macaroni and cheese, and collard greens.

She smiled at him. "From private plane and stretch limo to this. Was today too much? Are you reasserting your humble roots?"

"It's a tab I can afford."

"Well, no one ever said I was after you for your money." Vanity's eyebrows went up.

Dante showed no reaction.

"What's wrong?" she asked.

"Are you? Still after me, that is?"

Vanity's green eyes were less than candid. "I'm tired, Dante. We've flown to Mississippi and back, and I've just spent the last few hours helping Christina get settled at Max's."

"I think that's the longest 'no' I've ever heard."

She looked away, then back at him.

"I feel like you've had an important talk about us. Only I didn't get to hear it."

Vanity was silent.

"Everything was great until you went to your therapist on Sunday. Nothing's been the same since."

Her eyes dimmed. "Do you really think everything was so great?"

The food arrived, two heaping platters of death by carbohydrates.

But Dante's appetite had faded. Who wanted to eat like a pig *during* a breakup talk? Regardless, he grabbed an onion ring and wolfed it down, trying to move on in his head, hoping his heart could catch up later. He thought about Max's Pier speech.

It's easy to get caught up in being Vanity's boyfriend. I've roamed that jungle, and I got lost in it, too.

Dante shrugged at Vanity. the last thing he wanted to be was her K-Fed. "Well, the sex was great."

Vanity looked possibly offended. Apparently, she was still trying to decide.

"Fantastic," Dante clarified.

She grinned weakly. "It was more than that."

"What's better than fantastic?"

She rolled her eyes. "You know what I mean."

He nodded yes. "So why are you bailing then?"

"It's complicated."

"I've only had one year of private education, but I bet I can keep up."

Vanity smiled. "And I thought *I* had self-esteem problems. So far tonight, you're too poor *and* too stupid."

"Well, my mother has always said that you rich kids would ruin me."

She picked at her food, taking a few bites, but mostly moving it around. "Do you ever see any of your old friends? Or have we totally corrupted you?"

Dante thought about it. "Do you remember Vince? He used to be my best buddy."

Vanity gazed back at him blankly.

"He was with me on that night we first met. You were patrolling the door at Black Sand."

Her eyes sparkled with recognition. She nodded, grinning. "I didn't want to let him through, did I?"

"That's the one. Anyway, he got his girl pregnant, so he's been spending fifty hours a week managing a Subway for the last year." Dante sighed. "We drifted." He began to attack the macaroni and cheese. "I can't imagine a life like that."

"Like what?" Vanity asked.

"Settling at seventeen. Having to divert all your energy to the daily grind of responsibility before you have a chance to see what's out there, to dream a little bit. I admire him on one level. Most guys are selfish and don't give a shit. But he and I had similar upbringings. So Vince is doing the right thing. But then the right thing is a pathetic existence." He paused. "He doesn't love her. I don't think he even likes her. And he just turned eighteen." Dante tore into a chicken wing and looked at her. "I thought you were supposed to be telling me why we just broke up?"

"I need breathing room."

Dante gave her a curious glance. "Do I suffocate you?"

His tone told her that he didn't think so. If the answer was yes, then it was her problem, not his. But that was true of almost all "their" issues: they were really hers.

"You don't suffocate me. If anything, you make my air better. But I need to breathe on my own."

He nodded thoughtfully.

"The last thing I need right now is a relationship with a guy. I mean, I'm just getting to the point where I can have a relationship with myself that isn't completely dysfunctional."

He pointed at her, smiling. "You've been in therapy too long."

Vanity laughed. "Oh, I'm just getting started. I'll probably become one of those obscenely self-aware people who stays in analysis *forever*."

"Have you already broken up with me?" Dante asked. "Because *I'm* about to pull the plug here if you haven't."

Now they laughed together.

Vanity sipped the iced tea and winced. "Oh my God, that's awful. It's so sweet. *Ick*. It tastes like syrup."

Dante shook his head. "See, we were doomed anyway. I need a down-home girl. That's how tea is *supposed* to taste."

Playfully, Vanity stuck out her tongue. "This is fun. It doesn't feel weird to me. Does it feel weird to you?"

He gave her an easy shrug, Max's Vanity forecast on

the pier still ringing in his mind. It was true. Being involved with her became an all-consuming concept. And losing yourself just seemed a natural progression of that.

Dante Medina could not afford to be lost. Too much was at stake. In between errands and his other duties at Bogart Recording, Dante was allowed to take advantage of dead studio time. This gave him the chance to lay down tracks for his next song idea, which was to use Willie Nelson's country-and-western classic "My Heroes Have Always Been Cowboys" as a musical underbed for a hip-hop anthem Dante called "My Heroes Have Always Been Gangstas." Paired with the right artist, he knew it would be a monster.

"I want us to be friends," Vanity was saying. "I don't want things to be awkward. We've only got a month until graduation. I want all of us to have a blast. Don't you?"

"Just to be up front, I can't go without sex for a month, so there will be another girl in the picture soon." He grinned.

Vanity leaned forward, looked deeply into his eyes, and whispered seductively, "But I bet the thread count on her sheets won't be nearly as high as mine."

Dante smiled. "How about one last good-bye fu—"

Vanity cut him off. "Oh, you wish!"

"Well, then give me ten bucks, Miss Girl Interrupted. Because *friends* go Dutch."

"So this is it," Vanity murmured.

"For now." Dante smiled. "Who knows? You might come crawling back, begging me to give you another chance."

Vanity smiled. "And would you?"

"Maybe," Dante whispered. But his eyes were saying hell yes.

"I am broken, but I am hoping/Daughter to father, daughter to father/I am crying, a part of me is dying."

As the Lindsay Lohan track "Confessions of a Broken Heart" blasted from Pippa's iPod, she tried vaguely to read the lips of the man yelling in her face. Finally, she cut off the device, beyond irritated.

"Sweetheart, you didn't need a car service! You needed a *moving* service!"

Pippa stood there unaffected as the lumpy driver struggled with her Vuitton trunks and dumped them onto the sidewalk, directly in front of a kiosk for curbside baggage check-in.

Whatever. She *had* asked for an SUV. There was loads of room. The lazy oaf just didn't want to lift anything but a bloody fork.

He finished unloading the last trunk and let roar an exaggerated grunt, after which his hands went straight to his lower back, as if seriously injured.

"Oh, please!" Pippa cried. "Stop being such a spaz-motic. I have every intention of giving you a lovely tip for your trouble."

All of a sudden, he could stand up straight again. "The fare's seventy." He put out his chubby hand, dirty palm up.

Pippa slapped two crisp one-hundred-dollar bills into it. "More than you deserve!"

He grunted his thanks and took off.

Hoping for assistance, Pippa tried to make eye contact with one of the Delta agents, but all of them were absurdly busy with other travelers. She huffed. One of the luggage chaps should be delighted to handle her vintage Vuitton pieces, as opposed to the dodgy bags that most people tugged around.

In preparation for the wait, Pippa plopped down on one of the trunks and crossed her legs, smoothing out her black stretch tube skirt and adjusting the neckline of her white shawl-collar three-quarter-sleeve wrap jacket. Both were by Donna Karan.

If only everyone would dress up a bit for a trip—instead of lumbering about in tacky togs like a society of bus patrons—then the world might be a prettier place.

"And just where do you think you're going?" the familiar voice rang out.

Startled, Pippa turned. That's when she saw Max, impervious to the world, standing in front of his gleaming Porsche with his arms folded.

She looked away. "Las Vegas. Who knows? Maybe I'll take a job at the Bunny Ranch."

He strode toward her, cocky attitude in overdrive, acting like he owned not only the entire Miami International Airport, but the flight zone above it, as well. "Aren't you overdressed for the Bunny Ranch?"

Pippa made quite a show out of ignoring him, leaning down to adjust the leather ties on her Chloe platform wedges.

"I realize it's important to make a good first impression. But I think you're trying too hard."

A rush of anger rose up. Pippa could feel it burning on her cheeks. For sure he was a true Biaggi. Just like his father. Only a better version. And that made him so much worse.

"Fuck off, Max!" Pippa shouted.

All of a sudden, a man in a ghastly camp shirt and cheap khakis stepped into the fray, settling into a tough stance. "Is this guy bothering you?" He gestured to Max with an outstretched thumb.

But before Pippa could answer, Max was saying, "Actually, sir, she's the one bothering me."

Pippa did a pantomime to convey her disgust and annoyance.

Max smiled at her. "It's been that way for almost a year."

The concerned bystander, now with a more accurate read on the situation, left them to their teen drama. He moved on, muttering curses under his breath.

"It's true, you know," Max said.

Pippa betrayed no reaction.

Now he was standing in front of her. "I'm not any good at this."

She glanced up. "Be more specific, Max. As far as I know, you're not good at anything."

He nodded slowly, the impression lingering that he had shown up tonight prepared to take a few tough jabs. "Okay, I suck at a lot of things . . . like apologizing for anything wrong I've done . . . telling people I love how much I care about them . . . admitting that half the shit I say should probably just be ignored."

Pippa challenged him. "Only half?"

Max's shrug was the compromise. "Okay, maybe sixty percent. When I'm sober. If I'm hammered, that percentage might go up to eighty."

It killed her to do it, but this made Pippa crack a smile. She could feel herself thawing toward him. And the truth was, she missed Max immensely—the wild nights out, the endless talks on the phone, just the psychic comfort of having a best mate.

"Vanity told me everything," Max began quietly. "I'm sorry. I don't know what else to say. You got him pretty good, though. An irrevocable million-dollar trust? *Sweet.* The son of a bitch still controls mine. So I can't exactly sue him for emancipation. I guess I'll just go on hating him like always."

Pippa looked at him, her eyes gently admonishing. "Where are your principles?"

Max pointed to his Porsche. "I'm driving them. Do you want a ride?"

Pippa noticed a black SUV coast by, then speed up. She thought of Vinnie. A cold panic seized her. But just as quickly, the concern vanished. It couldn't be him. That SUV was an Escalade and he drove a Lincoln Navigator. She sighed her relief.

"You okay?" Max asked.

"I'm fine," Pippa insisted, waving a hand as if officially dismissing her old life and old fears. She stood up and fixed a helpless glance upon her precious trunks. "None of these will fit in your—"

Max cut her off. "Vanity warned me." He tossed a look backward, whistled, and pointed at the massive Vuitton pile.

A car honked in dutiful acknowledgment.

"Omar followed me in one of our trucks. He'll take care of that," Max explained. Then he pulled Pippa in for a fast embrace. "And I'll take care of you." He kissed her on the lips, slowly, softly, sweetly.

Pippa touched his face, smoothing out an unruly brow as she stared into his eyes. What she saw gazing back moved her deeply. It had nothing to do with sexual objectification. It had everything to do with love and respect. "Your secret's safe with me," she whispered.

"What secret?"

Pippa smiled at him. "That the brattiest bastard in Miami is the nicest guy around."

From: Bijou

Somebody's been shot.

10:03 pm 5/26/06

chapter fifteen

You swore those days were behind you," Dante said, hooking an arm around Max. "Yet here we are again."

"Dude, it's *graduation*. I had to do something. I mean, just look at them." He waved a hand over the energetic crowd at his Star Island mansion. "Can you imagine any of these jizzbags trying to pull off a big event? I did it for the kids, man. I did it for the kids."

Dante started to move away.

But Max held him back. "Dude, real quick, you see that girl over there in the corner tongue wrestling with the guy who looks like Nick Lachey? And I say that with a degree of hope. For all I know. it could actually *be* Nick Lachey."

Dante gave Max a curious look, wondering how many Buds had hit his brain. "Uh, dude, that's your sister."

Max sighed. "Yeah, I know. I'm thinking of putting her up for adoption. And then I remembered that you were an only child. So . . . you interested?"

Dante laughed. "Let me put it to you this way—I'd take on Chucky from those *Child's Play* movies as a little brother before I'd take on Sho as a little sister."

"Dude, I'm hurt."

Dante patted his cheek. "You'll get through it, bitch." And then he pressed through the crowd, alternately amazed and annoyed. Leave it to Max to host a MACPA pregraduation party with most of the guests not even being past, present, or future students at the school.

He felt a tug on his arm.

"Finally! Someone I actually know!" It was Christina. "This is insane!"

"No, it's *Max*," Dante corrected, protectively placing his hand in the small of her back and leading her to a less rowdy area.

Christina smiled gratefully.

Dante found a tiny patch of calm in a hallway leading into the library. He breathed a sigh of relief. "I think I'm getting too old for this. Could that be? I'm only seventeen." He shook his head wearily. "This is your house, too. You could send them home."

Christina laughed. "*My* house? I'm just an extended guest!"

Dante grinned. "Squatters have rights, too."

They stood there in easy silence, observing the chaotic scene, jamming to "SOS" by Rihanna.

"So have you answered the sixty-four-thousand-dollar question yet?" Dante asked.

Christina peered up at him. "About college?"

He nodded.

"I keep going back and forth. As of this moment, I *am* going to the Savannah College of Art and Design." One beat. "I think."

Dante pulled her in for a hug. "Go to college, girl. Don't be like the rest of us."

"Oh, so modest," Christina answered. "As if you're struggling, Mr. Prep School Gangsta."

Dante winked at her. The breakup with Vanity had been fortuitous. He put all of his energy back into his music and recorded a sick demo for "My Heroes Have Always Been Gangstas." Bogart Recording's owner had helped him navigate the legal waters to secure permission to sample the original track.

But Pippa had been the real secret weapon. After playing the track for the group during one of their many late nights in the Biaggi basement, Pippa touched on a brilliant strategy.

"You have to get this played at a strip club!" Pippa had insisted. "Forget radio. That's ancient. Besides, stations today are just corporate cogs in the wheel that only play what's already a hit. A good club DJ will take a chance on something new. If it's hot. Anyway, that's where all the hip-hop executives hang out. Those loons are just sitting around waiting for a lap dance. So why not start there?"

Dante had turned Pippa loose, and she had enlisted the help of LaTonya, formerly a dancer at Cheetah, but now taking it off at a club called Diamonds frequented by powerhouse industry vets like Jermaine Dupri, Dr. Dre, and Sean Combs. A week later Chamillionaire had agreed to record Dante's track and bring him in as a co-producer.

"Okay, I got lucky," Dante told Christina. "But college is still a smart move."

"I'm just not sure that I want to be shackled to books for four years down in Georgia. Part of me feels like I just started living my life. I want to continue that. Besides, you're not the only mogul in training."

Dante nodded impressively. The girl was definitely that. Christina had inked a deal with Viz Media to publish the first *Harmony Girl* collection, and Square Enix, the creators of *Final Fantasy*, were circling the project with designs on turning the *manga* into a video game.

Dante gave Christina a patronizing pat on the head

that he knew would drive her crazy. "You've come so far, Jap. I'm proud of you."

Christina practically stomped her feet. "I'll *never* get rid of that name!"

"Who *are* these loons?" Pippa demanded. "I've been upstairs. I've been downstairs. I've been room to room. They're all strangers. Are you sure we're at the right party?"

Vanity laughed. "Max's parties have *always* been like this. The problem is that we're sober for this one. Keep in mind, Max used to have birthday parties for people and not even invite them. It was just a good excuse for a big bash."

Pippa grumbled, looking around in semidistress. "And here I thought he was maturing so nicely. Now he's regressed back to being the party nitwit."

"I'm sure it's only a temporary setback brought on by graduation fever," Vanity mused. Then she watched with concern as a plastered girl was led upstairs by three guys who resembled anything but responsible chaperones.

Pippa saw the problem in motion and expelled a frustrated groan. "Our third save of the night! God, I feel like Batgirl!"

Vanity moved quickly to take down the situation, reaching the group just as they were shutting a bedroom door.

"Oh, shit! You again!" It was Dog Breath, a stocky minor league baseball player with buzzed hair and bad skin.

"My sentiments exactly," Vanity said coldly. "You should be on some national registry for party creeps."

Pippa blew past them, storming the room to seek out the girl.

Vanity followed close behind her, getting quite accustomed to their vigilante sisters routine. Now the task was to find a responsible friend to help this poor girl.

Pippa shot Dog Breath a look of disgust. "You know, if you'd invest in a simple bottle of Scope, then you might earn a more flattering nickname. The result could be hooking up with a girl who doesn't have to be unconscious to stick around."

"Why don't you mind your own business, bitch?" Another cretin from the group was mouthing off, this one a mean-looking drunk wearing a Toby Keith concert T-shirt and a baseball cap that read CUT HER FACE. How charming.

Vanity began to get nervous. This situation could easily spiral out of control.

But Pippa held her ground. "First of all, the only 'bitches' in the room are the three guys trying to take advantage of a girl who's obviously trashed and has no idea what's going on."

"Screw it, Ray," Dog Breath said. "Let's head out. This party's bullshit."

Vanity experienced a stirring sense of danger.

"I'm not listening to this bitch!" Ray yelled. "We didn't take advantage of anything. This girl wanted it."

" 'This girl' can barely say her own name!" Pippa roared. "And I'm quite sure that if she were capable of declaring her wants, it wouldn't be for three losers to have sex with her. One competent man can usually get the job done, *Ray*. Too bad you have to call in for reinforcements. Don't ever get married. Your honeymoon expenses will be outrageous."

Vanity bent down to retrieve the girl in question. She was slumped against the pillows, hardly able to stand up, a total rag doll that might puke at any moment.

Pippa moved in to assist, ignoring Ray's nasty stare as they took the girl out of the room and piloted her downstairs.

Max came dancing up, grooving to the endless Rihanna mix. "SOS" seemed to never end. "Who's your friend?"

Vanity glowered at the oblivious host. "Did you invite Dog Breath?"

Max recoiled at the suggestion. "Dog Breath doesn't get invited to anything, he just unfortunately shows up. Kind of like the human equivalent of mold. Where is he? I'll throw his ass out."

"He and his posse need to be tossed before somebody gets hurt," Vanity said sharply, pointing upstairs.

"Consider it done." Max marched off to play eviction cop.

Vanity and Pippa, still struggling with the girl, traded bemused glances.

"I can't judge her too harshly," Vanity said. "I've *been* her at parties like this."

"Same here. Maybe she'll get smart and sort herself out like we did. Until then, let's find out who she belongs to." Pippa let out a piercing whistle. "Does anyone *know* this soggy tramp?"

Vanity laughed, shaking her head. Oh, how far they had evolved.

Two young women stepped forward to make the claim on the mystery drunk, who happened to be named Jenna and was apparently studying communications at the University of Miami.

Vanity realized that Jenna represented her new target market. And there were legions of girls just like her out there waiting to be reached.

Mimi had assisted Vanity in strategizing a celebrity reinvention, an image light-years away from the superficial worlds of fashion modeling and appearances at special events.

The result had become an exciting and cathartic work

in progress. It was a collaboration with her therapist, Dr. Cleo Parker, on a book called *The Lost Girl Sessions*, a revolutionary approach to self-help that would juxtapose Vanity's most intimate journal writings with clinical observations and analysis by Dr. Parker.

The final product would be revealing in a manner that made Vanity constantly second-guess the project. But she knew that it could be a powerful tool to help girls all over America. So she was digging deep and doing the hard work.

There was something beautiful about *The Lost Girl Sessions*, because through the process of writing it, Vanity was finding herself. And it was a wonderful feeling.

Max huddled with Eli Gray, a three-hundred-pound linebacker for the Miami Dolphins and tonight's go-to guy for bouncing losers out of the mansion.

"I'm all over it, Max," Eli said, beaming an intense look at Dog Breath and his crew.

Max clapped a hand on the mountain that was Eli's shoulder. "You're a good man."

He ventured downstairs and caught sight of Christina inching her way through the crowd. "Jap!"

She looked at him balefully.

Max cut through the body crush, finally reaching her. "This party sucks!"

Christina laughed at him.

"And to think the five of us could be having an awesome dinner at Café Sambal right now."

She shrugged helplessly. "There's always San Loco."

Max nodded, vibing on the idea. The taco stand had become their regular late-night haunt. When the craving hit, even the finest South Beach restaurants couldn't beat the two-dollar beef hard shells for culinary bliss.

Max pushed toward the bar, pulling Christina along.

"I think there are at least five people here for every one MACPA student," Christina told him.

"I know," Max growled. "Somebody posted the details on MySpace." Making eye contact with the main bartender, he pretended to slice his neck with an index finger, then turned to Christina. "I just cut off the liquor. Most of these crashers will be gone in fifteen minutes."

Christina clutched his arm. "At least you'll get a good bit from this."

"Yeah." Max laughed. "You know what they say: Pain creates the best comedy."

Dante appeared and hooked an arm around Max's neck. "Dude, did you actually shut down the bar before midnight? I'm shocked. This has to be going against some sacred rich party-boy covenant."

"Yeah, it's right up there with inviting the maid's son."

Vanity and Pippa arrived just in time to catch the exchange and erupt with laughter.

"I'll be here all week," Max cracked, doing his best cheesy stand-up guy.

Word about the closed bar spread fast, and throngs of too-lit-to-quit revelers began spilling out of the Biaggi mansion.

A small crowd remained, but for the first time all night, it was manageable.

Max vaulted behind the bar. "Red Bull for everyone! We need fuel to make it all the way to San Loco." He tossed them out at a rapid clip, then raised the slim can for an impromptu toast.

His gaze swept over the faces of his friends . . . his gypsy family . . . his whole life. Emotion tugged at him. He was close to losing his composure.

"I can't believe it!" Pippa shouted. "Max Biaggi Jr. with bloody stage fright!"

Everybody laughed, Max included. She knew. Pippa had stepped in to save him from a teary breakdown. The girl could read him like a children's book.

Max cleared his throat and raised his Red Bull higher. "To getting through it all . . . high school, beach muggings, assaults on boats, sex tape scandals, car crashes, nervous breakdowns, crazy mothers, bastard fathers, wack-job cult camps, kidnappings, overdoses, breakups, strip club raids . . . have I left anything out?"

"Bad stand-up acts!" Dante shouted.

"And hip-hop wannabes!" Max finished, leaping atop the bar to drink deep and pump his fist in the air.

The sound of a single gunshot exploded, followed by screaming, hysteria, and general confusion.

Max froze.

In the center of the room, he saw a flash of metal as Dog Breath pushed away the hand of his buddy, the one wearing a CUT HER FACE baseball cap. They were supposed to be long gone. Why were they back?

Another scream. Closer. Louder. Heart-stopping.

It was Vanity.

Max tracked the terrified look in her eyes. What he saw next made him go weak with anguish.

Christina was crying.

Staggering off the bar, he felt big tears form in his eyes as the terror broke through. A cold sweat slicked his body as he went down on both knees.

Pippa lay on her back. Her eyes were open. Blood pumped from a hole in the center of her chest.

Dante was calling for an ambulance.

But Max knew that it was too late. He cradled Pippa's head, her eyes calm as she coughed up blood in a final body spasm, calmer still as a dead look glazed over them.

The beginning of the agony rushed through him. When Max spoke, it was in the tiny voice of a child.

"She's gone."

From: Bijou

What will become of them?

10:37 am 5/27/06

epilogue

a Piaggia on South Pointe Drive gave off ultrahot vibrations—Miami style. The floor was sand. The banquettes were striped yellow and white. The umbrellas were shocking orange. And the power lunches ruled.

The reservation had originally been for five.

Vanity discreetly gestured to the waiter to remove the fifth place setting. Seeing it on the table only intensified the traumatic reality that Pippa was not with them.

The heartbreak seemed magnified by the fact that a postceremony graduation brunch at this restaurant had been her idea. In fact, it was the sole reason that the group had conjured up the strength to gather. In tribute to Pippa.

Vanity observed as Dante cut a hostile glance and shifted uncomfortably in his seat. She tracked his gaze, noticing an older gentleman at a nearby table watching him with keen interest.

"I think you're being cruised," Max said, picking up on the distraction while turning his third mimosa upside down. "He wants you to be his boy toy." It was classic Max, but his voice rang hollow. The zing was gone.

Vanity could tell that he had been crying.

Dante worked hard to ignore the stranger's attention.

Thoughtfully, Christina fingered the stem of her champagne flute.

Vanity's mimosa remained untouched. She reached for her water glass just as Dante's admirer approached the table.

"Forgive me, I've been staring relentlessly since you walked in." The man was polished, well-groomed, impeccably dressed, and, quite obviously, a *confirmed bachelor*. "I have to ask. Are you an actor?"

Dante shook his head no.

Vanity watched the scene unfold.

The man presented Dante a business card and launched into a breathless pitch. "I'm an agent with Meteor. You've got the perfect look for the lead role in a script that's the hottest property in Hollywood. Call me next week. I'd like to fly you out for a screen test. See how the camera responds to you." A manicured hand was offered. "Sky Shamblin."

"Uh . . . Dante Medina." He shook fast.

Sky flashed a superwhite smile. "Great name." And then he was gone.

Max could hardly contain himself. He scrambled to inspect the card. "Dude, Meteor's *huge*. Sky Shamblin's *huge*. Last year he turned down my father for representation."

Dante just sat there, stunned.

"I guess this means we're both heading to L.A.," Max said.

"Yeah," Dante murmured. "I guess so."

"Don't forget me," Christina put in.

Max tilted his head. "Brush up on your geography, Jap. Last time I checked, Savannah was in Georgia, not California."

"I'm not going," Christina announced. "I sent the email turning down the scholarship this morning."

Vanity, Dante, and Max all turned on her in alarm.

"It just doesn't feel right."

Everybody nodded their understanding.

"Well, that makes three of us," Max remarked.

Vanity felt under siege as everybody probed her face with meaningful looks that begged the question: Would she join them in Los Angeles?

Surreptitiously, Vanity slipped her right hand underneath the table and palmed her belly. Her period was three weeks late. The pregnancy test was positive. Dante was the baby's father. And Vanity had no idea what she was going to do about it. Telling him was out of the question. He had big dreams to pursue, and no way was she going to stand in the way of that.

"God, this is strange," Max remarked softly. "Pippa just died last night. And here we are making plans."

A mournful silence hit the table.

"How can life be going on already?" Max asked.

"Because it does," Vanity whispered, thinking about the life that had ended . . . and also about the life that was growing inside her. "The lamest clichés are the truest ones. Life goes on."

Dear Readers,

I hope you enjoyed *Beautiful Disaster*, the third book in my new FAST GIRLS, HOT BOYS series. It was excruciating to write Pippa's death scene. Truth be told, by the time I approached the end, I didn't want *anyone* to die. But, alas, somebody had to perish. And in this case, it was the darling British tart.

I've been thrilled by the many wonderful letters from readers. People have truly enjoyed the cliffhanger elements of this trilogy and the fun of anticipating the next installment.

Normally, I write books from a detailed outline, but for this series, I employed a much more organic approach by just sitting down with a blank yellow legal pad and letting the characters tell the story. Perhaps that's why these books have been so exciting. I had no idea what was going to happen, either!

If you can't get enough of FAST GIRLS, HOT BOYS, then visit my official website at www.readkylie.com for free reader extras. There's an exclusive three-part short story called "Jailbait," which is a prequel focusing on Max's not-so-baby sister, Shoshanna, the ultimate wild child. She's fifteen going on twenty-one. The first chapter was posted with the release of *Cruel Summer*, the second chapter was posted in tandem with *Bling Addiction*, and the finale is available now. I hope you enjoy "Jailbait."

The second extra is a free Podcast available for immediate download on iTunes. This multisegment radio show is packed with a few spoilers on *Beautiful Disaster*, cool information about Miami, plus dish on the latest fashion and trends. Just log on to iTunes and type "Kylie Adams" or "Fast Girls, Hot Boys" into the Podcast search engine. At no charge you can download the program and subscribe to future Podcasts. There's also a *Beautiful Disaster* iMix available on iTunes. Just log on and type "Beautiful Disaster" into the iMix search engine. You'll see a fun playlist featuring songs and artists mentioned in the book. This is part three of the soundtrack to the lives of Vanity, Dante, Max, Pippa, and Christina.

Wait—there's more! On my website, take a moment to join the K-List, otherwise known as "Kylie's Inner Circle." There's a special sign-up tab for fans of Fast Girls, Hot Boys. I'll be sending out periodic emails on the miniseries, future writing projects, and site updates. And don't forget to post me a K-Mail. I love hearing from readers, and I'm dying to know what you think about *Beautiful Disaster*!

With all good wishes,

Kylie Adams
www.readkylie.com

ıth is the new gıaı
list Goth girl wakes
me Goth and she's

LD LIFE CAR
la to life in the sp
'ear-old from Miam
1 Superstar? And d

IMER ALEX [
what he did this
; *Cape Fear* when ɛ
ıtion on North Carc

IICTION KYLI

As many as 1 in 3 Americans
have HIV and don't know it.

TAKE CONTROL.
KNOW YOUR STATUS.
GET TESTED.

To learn more about HIV testing,
or get a free guide to HIV and
other sexually transmitted diseases.

www.knowhivaids.org
1-866-344-KNOW